BACK TO THE
BEACH COTTAGE

ALSO BY JOANNE DEMAIO

Back to the Beach Cottage

A NOVELLA

Joanne DeMaio

To Hatchett's Point

A tucked-away Connecticut beach,
wild and true.

one

Six Months Later
— January —

A LONE PICKUP TRUCK DRIVES along the main drag. The night is still, and wispy clouds pass in front of a crescent moon. There's a coldness, too, that settles like a fog on everything. Storefronts' softly illuminated windows are frosted. Dry, sweeping marsh grasses bend beneath the weight of frozen dew crystals in saltwater inlets. Those coastal Connecticut bays are fringed with thin ice. Jagged pieces edge the calm seawater.

The man in the pickup clutches the steering wheel with gloved hands. He leans forward, his shoulders hunched against that cold—even with the heat blowing from the dashboard vents. A sherpa-lined beanie covers his head; a down-filled vest covers his thick flannel shirt. The truck's headlights cut through the

1

darkness as the vehicle passes the deserted sights without slowing up.

Not until the driver turns off onto a nearly hidden dirt road.

He seems to relax then, this man. You can tell by the way he sits back with a long breath. The dirt road winding through dense woods seems familiar to him. As the truck shifts over frost heaves, the man easily rounds the bends in the road. His headlights reflect off a *Dead End* sign mounted on a tree. Gone are the closed-up little shops and eateries he'd just driven past. Gone are the buttoned-up homes with lamplit windows. The white chapel. The garden center. The empty harbors.

Now? Now, towering trees line his night view—as far as the eye can see. The trees lean in over the road. They form a tunnel of sorts, beneath which he keeps driving. The bare branches reach high above, looking like tatted lace against the moonlit sky. That moon drops just enough light to cast the night in pale shadow. Everything is a silhouette against the scant illumination: the spindly trees, the scrappy roadside brush, a neglected shanty in the woods.

Black, black. As the man looks out the windshield, everything is dappled in shades of black. His truck jostles over another heave in the packed dirt, then continues on deeper into the darkness, into the forest. The only sound is that of his tires on the snow-dusted road—crunching fallen twigs, humming over the hardened earth.

Until finally, the vehicle rounds one last curve—and the night opens up.

The forest is behind him now. And ahead, a black sky reaches east to west and deep to the horizon. Tiny stars glimmer against that sky. They almost pulse against the darkness. The man driving slows the vehicle and takes in the sight. He opens his window, too. Quickly—with some urgency. As he drives, he leans close to that night air and sharply inhales. Because beneath that vast black sky lies a sea just as black on this cold night. But the salt air rises all the same, and the man's chest rises with another breath of it.

More silhouettes, then, in the night. An old painted house sitting on the left. And cottages—shingled cottages mere shadows on expansive lawns. The trees now are few, but just as imposing in the yards. Rising tall, those trees' outstretched branches keep sentry over the few cottages lining this long dirt road to Hatchett's Point.

Finally, the man turns his pickup into a driveway that's nothing more than packed-down lawn. The driveway leads to a rambling, one-story cottage with a sloped roof. He parks outside the garage, shuts off the truck and takes another breath. The truck engine clicks as it cools down. And the man, well, he sits there and looks long at the place. At the empty rose trellis beside a paned window. Only frozen, twig-like branches cling to the trellis now. He looks at the weathered cottage itself. It's dark; no lights are on. Every window is as black as the night.

3

Bending low to see out the windshield, the man whispers, "*Been a long time.*"

~

But he doesn't go inside.

Something keeps the man sitting in his pickup truck. He leans back, pulls off his gloves and tosses them on the empty passenger seat. Shoves his beanie in his vest pocket, too, and runs his hand through his messed, dark hair. In a moment, he grabs his cell phone from the console and makes a call.

"Tommy. I'm here. At the beach cottage," he says, still looking at it through the windshield.

"Good, Mack. That's good. How was traffic?"

"Dead for a Friday."

"Typical off-season?"

"Yeah. So I'll take care of the place before the storm hits. Got the list Dad jotted down for me. Bought one of those electric snow shovels for the deck, too."

"That'll help," Tommy tells him. "Old Lyme's going to get clobbered. They're calling for a ton of snow at the shore there."

"No shit. I had groceries delivered at home and brought them with me. So the cottage fridge will be well stocked. And hey. Be sure to clear the parking lot at the warehouse. There's extra rock salt in the garage there, too. Put it down on the walkways."

"Will do, bro. Don't worry. You remember to take

4

those extra snow stakes? They sent too many—don't need all those lining our parking lot."

"Yeah," Mack says, glancing toward the bed of his pickup. "I grabbed a pile."

"Use them in the driveway there," Tommy tells him. "Maybe put some on that dark road. Help guide people through, the plow driver included."

"Okay." Mack leans forward, looking out at the cottage first, then off toward Long Island Sound in the distance. "Listen, Tommy. I might not make it to work Monday, either. Cover for me?"

"Sure, man. I'll finish upholstering those dining room chairs you started in the shop."

"Appreciate it. I'll maybe be here a couple of days. You know, wait out the storm to stay on top of things. Big nor'easter's coming. Don't need this old cottage to sink under the snow."

Finally, Mack puts on his sherpa-lined beanie, grabs his gloves and gets out of the truck. He looks left, at the dark cottage. Then right, toward Long Island Sound again. Tips his head up, too. And just breathes.

Apparently, he also makes a decision. Because next he walks alongside the cottage and cuts across the backyard. There's just enough pale moonlight to illuminate the frosty lawn sloping to a bank of dune grasses. In the midst of them, a sandy path winds to the beach. Mack pauses at the path's entrance, then makes his way through. The dried-out dune grasses are still. They don't sway and whisper, like in the summer warmth. Instead, the long grass blades are frozen. When Mack steps on some in the path, the grass snaps beneath his hiking boots.

The same is true on the beach. Winter's cold has toughened the sand. His boots don't sink into the soft grains, but walk hard on the surface. Still, no matter the season, the waves lap easy at shore. Mack walks along the night beach. It's cold and his step is brisk. He finally stops at the water and just stands there, alone. Looks down the length of the beach, too. Though it's empty, people *are* around. They're inside, settled into many of the nine cottages lining the long dirt road to the sea. His gaze moves to the headland jutting out into the Sound, and to the lone cottage on that elevated rise. Lights shine in the cottage windows. Behind him, he takes in the sight of more golden windows. Here, there … scattered in the darkness.

Only *his* cottage is invisible in the night. Only his is black.

Waves lap onshore near his booted feet. They splash on the sand and hiss back into the sea. Shoving his gloves into his back pocket, he quickly takes a few steps right into the shallows. While standing there, seawater swirls around his boots. He bends and sweeps his fingertips through the water, lifting a handful of the sea and tossing it up to the sky, toward that moon, in a thousand little droplets. Then he presses his fisted hands to his mouth and blows warm air on them before putting on his gloves, flipping up his vest collar and heading back.

⌒

Now, everything happens quickly. Once at his cottage, Mack right away unloads the storm gear from his truck bed: a new snow shovel; a bag of sand; ice scrapers. He leaves those on the deck for the night and brings the rest—grocery bags, a few packed cardboard boxes and a duffel—through the slider into the kitchen.

The cottage is just as dark inside as out. So after setting down the last carton, he flicks on a light. Blue stoneware lines the shelves near the sink. A basket of dried wildflowers and beach grasses sits on the kitchen table. A blue teakettle is on the stove. Mack glances around before putting away the groceries—opening and closing the refrigerator; stocking cabinet shelves. That done, he takes the cartons he'd hefted in and lines them against a side wall in the dining room. Hangs his vest and hat on a hook near the slider, too. All that's left then is his duffel, which he grabs up. After shutting off the kitchen light, he finally walks toward the bedroom.

But once in the dark hallway, he stops. Just stops there, heavy duffel in hand. Head dropped.

And slowly turns back. In the living room, he

switches on a floor lamp and sets down that duffel. Adjusts the wall thermostat. His every move is quiet. His step, soft. When he returns to the hallway, it's only to get a pillow and warm blanket from a closet there. He spreads that blanket on the couch, then unzips his duffel for his night things—pajamas, toothbrush and such—which he brings to the bathroom.

Some fatigue shows when he eventually returns to the living room. Wearing a heavy thermal top over flannel pajama bottoms, there's a change. His step slows. He drags a hand across his whiskered jaw. A paned window seems to draw him, the way he keeps glancing over at it. Once he shuts off the lamp, that's where he ends up—standing at that window. He moves aside the straight curtain and looks out on the winter night. Looks toward Long Island Sound. The crescent moon rises high above it in the black sky.

Dropping the curtain, Mack turns to the couch. As he settles in there, he pulls up the blanket and lies back on the pillow. His arms are crossed behind his head. The only sound is of heat ticking through the radiators.

In the dark living room, Mack looks up at the ceiling, then toward that same window again. *"Been a long time,"* his voice barely whispers.

two

VERY EARLY SATURDAY MORNING, YOU can hear the cold. It comes in the sound of wind. A brisk breeze lifts off Long Island Sound and whistles across the dips and valleys of the cottage yard. In the darkness before sunrise, Mack sits up on the living room sofa and turns on the floor lamp.

Around him now is all lightness. All white. On the painted walls. The white sofa. The painted end tables. The white-painted built-in dining room cupboards. White, white, white. When he closes his eyes against it, it's with some pained effort. He's forcing his eyes closed, obvious in his wince—as if he's not used to the lightness. As if his recent life's actually been dark.

As if he doesn't trust what he sees.

Until he throws off his blanket and gets to his duffel; gets to the day. He showers, skips a shave, and changes into jeans and another warm flannel shirt. The way he's moving around the quiet cottage, it seems like there's much to be done. In the kitchen, while the coffee's

9

brewing, he slices a bagel and drops the halves into the toaster. Behind him, sliding glass doors face the deck outside, and the backyard. It's really early. Morning's twilight only scarcely lightens the sky.

When that bagel pops in the toaster, Mack lifts a half and sees how lightly it's toasted. So he adjusts the dial to a much darker setting and presses the lever down again. And stands there, waiting. When wisps of smoke curl from the toaster a minute later, he pops up the lever, gingerly grabs out the charred bagel halves and tosses them hot into the sink. Oh, and he's uttering something, too.

"*Shit*," Mack whispers.

Bending over the counter and resetting the toaster dial once more—nudging it lighter, just a smidge—he then tries again with a second bagel. When that one pops up nicely toasted, his words are kinder. "*That'll do*," he tells himself while slathering on cream cheese and sitting alone at the kitchen table.

His aloneness in the kitchen doesn't seem to bother him much. Methodically, he digs into that bagel, one bite after another. As soon as one mouthful is swallowed, he begins on another. There's no magazine opened on the table for him to read. No newspaper headline from *The Day*, recapping the Connecticut stats and positivity rate of the pandemic. The TV is off, too. Mack doesn't scan his phone for emails or voicemails. He simply sits at the table and eats. Afterward, he washes his dishes at the sink before pouring a cup of hot coffee. That he takes into the living room, where he stops at the window facing the distant sea. Moving aside the straight curtain, he looks outside while sipping his coffee. The eastern horizon shows the first hint of light before sunrise.

So the day's just beginning. And not a minute's to be wasted, apparently. Because as he finishes his coffee, Mack returns to the kitchen and pulls his warm beanie on over his wavy, dark hair. Slips into his olive-green puffer vest, too. After dumping the last drops of coffee into the sink, he pulls a crumpled piece of paper from his vest pocket and flattens it on the countertop.

Quietly, he whispers a few of the random phrases scrawled there. "*Clear gutters. Shut off outside water. Cover deck furniture.*" He glances outside to the deck. "Guess I'll start there," he says, shoving the paper into his vest pocket again.

⁓

There's a shed out back. A good-sized beach shed with shingles that match the cottage's. Mack opens the shed's door and when he pulls a dangling string, a bare light-bulb fixture illuminates the space. It's dusty in there, and dank from sea damp. It's the kind of cold dank that gets you to wrap your arms in front of you— which Mack does as he looks around. Old bicycles lean against a side wall. Sun-bleached sand chairs hang from hooks on the back wall. Yard equipment—a lawn mower, leaf blower and edger—fill much of the shed space. Grilling supplies do, too. There's a charcoal grill, cans of lighter fluid, a half-empty bag of briquettes. Spatulas and tongs hang from a rack above the grill.

But no furniture covers are in sight.

Mack scans the space before turning and glancing behind him. He goes outside and lifts the lid of a wicker deck storage box. It's filled with various seat cushions, a watering can, badminton racquets. But no furniture covers for the deck table and chairs.

When Mack looks around, a sudden motion at the neighboring cottage catches his eye. An older man, maybe in his fifties, hurries from his curbside newspaper box back across the lawn. He's tall, thin, and a little grizzled looking—not having shaved yet. And the long wool coat he wears over his pajamas blows in the stiff sea breeze.

"How you doing, Mr. Hotchkiss?" Mack calls out.

"Hey, Mack! I'm good, good." This Mr. Hotchkiss veers Mack's way, stopping about ten feet from the deck. "Been a long time! Happy to see you back in these parts."

"Have to batten down the hatches here this weekend. Snow's coming."

"That it is." Mr. Hotchkiss folds that newspaper and clutches it close. "And how about yourself?" he asks, taking a step closer and looking with concern at Mack. His voice drops, too. "Doing okay?"

"Yeah, you know." Mack tugs up his vest against the

blowing wind. "So, hey. How was that New Year's recital of yours last week? Sorry I missed it this year."

"You didn't. It was rained out."

"That's right! I hear the coastline got swamped. This New England weather, man."

Mr. Hotchkiss holds his wool coat closed. "I've been doing that piano recital for twenty years now. In my living room, every single year. Always give an open invitation to the folks here at Hatchett's Point. Leave the Christmas lights up. And the tree. We build a fire in the fireplace. Serve hors d'oeuvres. Cheese and crackers. S'mores. But ... things were a little different this year."

"How so?"

"Well, guests can't come indoors with the pandemic, so me and my son got the piano out to the sunporch. Opened the windows so people could hear the music. Rigged up an amp, even. Set up some chairs all spaced out in the yard. Stocked the firepit. The works. Cleared the patio for anyone wanting a dance or two. Even bought fleece blankets for the guests. And then it rained buckets."

"Aw, you went all out, Mr. Hotchkiss. The whole nine yards." Mack shakes his head. "Too bad it didn't happen."

"Not really, because funny thing ... The recital's rescheduled for tonight, actually." When the wind kicks up again, the man turns against it and heads toward his own cottage. "So if you hear some melodies all day," he calls out, "it's just me fine-tuning the setlist."

"Concert's *tonight?*" Mack glances up at the cloudy sky. "You'll beat the storm, at least, before the snow starts flying later on."

Mr. Hotchkiss turns again and walks slowly backward. Strands of his hair lift in the wind as he squints over at Mack. "You oughta come. We've missed you here, Mack."

"Well. I'm not really sure," Mack tells him.

"Think about it," Mr. Hotchkiss calls as he backs closer to his cottage. "I know things have been tough on you, and with Avery—"

As he talks, Mack's ringing cell phone interrupts. He pulls it from his jeans pocket. "I got to take this, Mr. Hotchkiss," he says while lifting the phone. "It's my dad."

"Old man Martinelli? You give him my regards," Mr. Hotchkiss says before waving him off and hurrying back across his lawn—folded newspaper in hand, coat collar flipped up.

⌒

Mack turns away, walking toward the shed again. "Glad you called, Dad," he says into the phone. "Sorry I never got to your list sooner."

"Ah. No worries, son."

"With everything going on, I never had the chance." Mack glances across the backyard sloping to Long Island Sound in the distance. "Feels like a lifetime ago since me and Avery stayed here last summer."

"I can imagine, Mack. But it's a big help you're there now."

"Yeah, no problem."

"Hey, listen. Before I forget, your brother says he'll swing by your house and get the driveway cleared after the storm. So you don't have to worry about that. About going back and forth this weekend."

"Sounds good, Dad. Tell Tommy thanks, would you? Because now?" In a sudden gust of wind, Mack opens the shed door again. "Now I really have to get to that list of yours."

"Be sure to clear out those gutters."

"I know, I know. But first, where are the covers for the deck furniture?"

"In the shed. Top shelf, in back."

Mack walks through the shadowy space, around a wheelbarrow, past the push broom. "Above the sand chair hooks?" he asks, opening a plastic tote there. "Okay. Got 'em, Dad."

⌒〜

But even after bringing the storage tote to the deck; and after brushing off the furniture with his gloved hand; and after pushing the deck chairs in close to the table; and while sweeping away dry leaves swirling on the deck, something seems to be on Mack's mind. Something distracting him.

15

Because he keeps looking over toward the large paned windows of the sunporch at Mr. Hotchkiss' cottage.

While lifting the furniture covers from the tote, and securing them to the table and chairs, he's still bothered by whatever's on his mind. Why else, after tugging a vinyl cover over only half the table, would Mack stop? Yes, he stops, pulls out a chair and sits alone at the partially covered table. Sits hunched in his sherpa-lined beanie and down vest and looks out at the barren winter yard.

Does something else, too. He pulls his phone from his pocket and scrolls to a *Honeymoon Album* in his photos tab. Flicking through a few pictures, he stops on one taken here last June. It's a photograph of him and Avery slow-dancing on the stone patio behind the cottage one night. Avery wears a gray-and-white striped top over frayed khaki shorts. Her head rests on his shoulder. With one hand, Mack touches her sandy blonde hair; with his other, he grabs the shot. On the deck behind them, shimmering globe candles are scattered about. Half-filled wineglasses sit on the table. A wildflower bouquet spills from a white pitcher there, too.

But the way Mack looks now from that photograph to Mr. Hotchkiss' cottage—once, and then again—it's obvious. The *only* reason he and Avery would be dancing right there in the yard is Mr. Hotchkiss' famous piano playing. The neighbor's cottage windows must've

16

been thrown open that summer night, with melodic piano notes floating across the salt air.

And Mack must've reached for his bride's hand and asked for a dance beneath the moonlight. The stars above must've shined on their waltz as some melancholy song reached them, and as they gently swayed together. As they whispered soft words, and shared a long kiss.

Because from the looks of Mack now—from the way his finger brushes the picture on his cell phone, and from the way he sits back with a deep breath of that salt air lifting off the sea?

That one night must've been the sweetest of the whole, entire summer.

three

DONE, DONE, DONE."

Mack utters the words with a glance up at the early dawn sky. Then he checks the buckle straps and drawstring hem of the waterproof furniture covers. All's good and snug over the deck table and chairs.

With that task finished, he reaches into his vest pocket for his father's crumpled chore list—which promptly blows out of his fingers and tumbles willy-nilly across the expansive lawn. Mack gives quick chase, hurrying off the deck and alongside the cottage to the front yard. He runs this way and lurches that way as the wind tosses his list. His wool beanie blows off, too. And at one point, he almost trips. His hand touches the ground, though, and he regains his balance. And reaches for the elusive list. Then reaches again, farther.

"*Got it!*" he says, straightening and clutching the wayward slip of paper. Grabs his hat off the frozen lawn, too. Which is when he notices something odd and does a double take. Then he veers across the dirt

18

road to where a lone piece of furniture sits at the curb. It looks like a vintage blanket chest. But there's more. There's a sign taped to the front. The sign reads: *FREE! TAKE IT.* Mack checks out the chest's seat cushion. Its faded sage-colored fabric is threadbare and distressed. He lifts that upholstered lid and a slight cedar scent rises from inside the empty chest. Giving his head a slow shake, he closes the lid and brushes his gloved hand across it. As he does, a sudden noise gets him to look up. A woman stands in a window of the cottage there. She's in her late sixties, maybe; her light brown hair is bobbed; she wears a bathrobe tied at the waist.

And she's rapping on the windowpane. When she sees Mack look up, her smile is warm; her wave, happy.

"Rosa!" Mack steps toward the closed window. He waggles his finger at her and motions to the chest.

Problem is, Rosa is talking to him—like she's explaining something—but Mack can't hear her through the window glass. You can tell by the way he squints and tips his head.

"*What?*" he asks, stepping across the frozen lawn and getting closer to the window.

Rosa motions for him to wait, and returns holding a mini whiteboard and black marker. She's also busy jotting something down. As she does, Mack tells himself, "I'll have to remember that. The pandemic's got everyone finding new ways to safely communicate."

Suddenly, another window-knock. When Mack

looks over again, Rosa holds up her sign for him to read—smiley face drawn there, too.

"*Glad to see you here. Been a long time,*" Mack reads to himself, and nods in agreement.

Rosa erases the words and scrawls some more.

"*Chest was set near a window,*" Mack reads on. "*Cushion sun-faded now. And Rafe spilled coffee on it.*"

Finally, after erasing *those* lines, she writes, *Had a good run, but it's done.*

When Mack looks at Rosa, she shrugs. "Done?" he asks his neighbor.

Rosa quickly wipes off her board. *Old*, she writes then.

"But *old* furniture's the best," Mack shouts outside the window. "*Old*-world craftsmanship. Dovetail construction. And it has a seat rail! Rosa, this chest's a quality piece."

Rosa diligently writes more before turning her sign of black-marker words. *All worn out*, they say.

Mack stands right at her window now. Only thin panes of glass separate them as his voice gets stern. "Don't you know who your neighbors are? The Martinellis!" He glances back at the weary blanket chest. "And it's Martinelli Upholstering to the rescue."

Rosa? Well, no sign's necessary now. She simply smiles and gently pats her heart.

"Rosa," Mack says. "Hang on two minutes."

He doesn't wait for her answer, either. Instead, he turns on his heels and trots across the street to his cottage. Running around back, he goes inside through the slider and hurries to the end of the long hallway. The room there is obviously an off-site workroom for Martinelli Upholstering. A sewing machine is set up on a long table. Spools of upholstery thread and pins and fabric measuring tapes are scattered there, too. On the wall, fabrics of every color and texture fill several shelves. A large white basket sits on the floor.

"Perfect," Mack says, lifting the empty basket and dropping a handful of fabric samples into it.

In no time, Mack's back outside at Rosa's window.

"Pick one." He lifts a piece of fabric, this one blue with veins of gold thread running through it, and holds it close to the shut window. "One?" Mack calls out. Next is a gold-dotted green velour. "Two?" Setting that back in the basket, he lifts another swatch—stripes in various earth tones. "Three?"

And so it goes as Mack works through his samples of tweed and plain and floral; espresso and gray heather and gold; numbers four and five and six.

Rosa hesitates, then jots a number on her whiteboard.

"One?" Mack asks.

I like the blue, Rosa writes, drawing a few ocean-wave lines on her board.

"Okay." A sudden gust of wind gets Mack to look

up as the rising sun slowly brightens the sky. "I'll be back later to fix up that cushion for you." He starts walking backward. "Got to clear the gutters first, before the snow comes." He turns to jog away, calling over his shoulder, "Don't let anyone take that chest!"

As he crosses the dirt road, Mack glances again at the morning sky. Twilight finally gives way to sunup. Once inside his cottage, he stops at the kitchen counter, sets down the basket of fabric samples and starts a fresh pot of coffee brewing. He also pulls his father's crumpled list from his vest pocket. Standing there, Mack adds one more task on that list—after checking his watch as though gauging if there's enough time for *all* his tasks.

"*Reupholster chest cushion,*" he whispers while scrawling the words.

⁓

Walking out the slider to the deck, Mack stops at the railing. He's facing the sun rising over the distant winter beach. Anyone would stop there, gloved hands on the railing, eyes to the east. The colors in the January sky are that dramatic. That rising sun casts a swath of red over the slate-blue sea. A bank of thin clouds are rolling in, too, out over the water.

Mack doesn't stand there long, though. His hand pats that vest pocket holding his crumpled task list— almost like a reminder—and he gets back to the shed.

When he gives the dangling light string a tug, the bare bulb flicks on. Mack looks around until he spots the ladder hung horizontally on big wall hooks. Heading that way, he says under his breath, *"Shame we couldn't get this place in order in the fall."*

Looks like he still won't get the place in order. Or at least, not the gutters. Not with the charcoal grill in his way. When he moves it aside, he first shakes his head with a long breath. And second? Second, he pulls his cell phone from his jeans pocket again and opens that *Honeymoon Album* in the photos tab. These days, anything seems to spark a memory for him. And you can see how he doesn't fight it. No, he instead gives himself over to whatever memory beckons.

Because standing alone in the cold, dusty shed, Mack scrolls through the pictures now until he finds a photograph of Avery. Her blonde hair is side-parted. Small gold hoops hang from her ears. She's sitting in a faded webbed chair on the lawn last June. And there it is—the grill. It's situated in front of her. Smoldering charcoal briquettes in its grate fade from black to gray.

"Really got to know you that evening," Mack whispers, as though Avery's right there with him. As though he's talking right to her. As though he wants to just touch her soft hair. Stroke her face with the back of his fingers.

"Knock, knock!" a man calls out from beyond the shed doorway. He's older, about seventy, with graying hair. He wears corduroy pants, and a scarf is wrapped

23

around the upturned collar of his zipped-up jacket. A face mask covers his mouth and nose.

Mack spins around to see the man. And anyone, Mack included, can't miss from the man's smiling eyes that he's so happy to see Mack. "Rafe," Mack says.

"Mack! It's been a long time. Got a few minutes to catch up?"

"Sure." Mack looks from Rafe to his cell phone. "Been meaning to get out there and clear the gutters. But ... well, you caught me in a memory, that's all," Mack explains before setting his phone on a dusty table. "Hang on, let me grab a mask," he says, reaching into a small box beside the hedge trimmers on a shelf. "My dad uses these when he does yard work. Allergies, you know?" Mack asks while looping the mask strings over his ears beneath his beanie. "Who would've thought we'd be using them like this now?"

The whole time, Rafe's been quiet. It's almost like he's just letting Mack talk. Letting him say anything on his mind; anything he's feeling. Rafe just watches Mack with kind eyes.

Mack must sense it as he picks up his phone. Because he starts to put it back in his pocket, but glances at the photo on the screen once more. "I was just looking at a picture. Of Avery," he says.

"Can I see?" Rafe walks closer to the shed. Just a step or two, then stops.

Mack, looking at the photo of Avery sitting near the smoldering grill, gives a nod. He holds up the phone so

Rafe can see the picture. "We really got to know each other, me and Avery. Sitting around the grill one day last summer, on our honeymoon here," Mack explains. He looks at the picture again. "Avery had a list of questions to test how much I knew about her, and vice versa. You know, guess each other's favorite food. And as kids, what we wanted to be when we grew up. Things like that."

Rafe nods. "The good stuff," he says, still only watching Mack.

"Sure. The questions got serious, too. Like … we had to guess when the other was last happy. And one question, Rafe? Oh man, it really got to me."

"What was it?"

"I'll tell you. We had to guess each other's biggest fear. Problem was, I really didn't know *mine*. Couldn't fathom *what* I was most afraid of. So after Avery ventured a guess, I couldn't answer her that night." Mack puts his cell phone back in his jeans pocket. "But don't I know the answer now," he admits with a regretful laugh. His voice is quiet when he reveals it. "Life *without* Avery."

From a safe distance, Rafe shakes his head. "Helluva road you've travelled these past months, Mack."

"Yeah." Mack drags a hand down his jaw. "Well," he says, turning to that ladder hanging on the wall then. "So how've you and Rosa been?"

"Oh, the same. Fine, fine. Just laying low, staying safe."

"I hear you. You know I stopped by your place a while ago?"

"Rosa told me. About that blanket chest, I guess?"

"That's right. The one Martinelli Upholstering will get all gussied up for you."

"Rosa always did like that little chest." Rafe pulls his wallet from his pocket. "So how much do I owe you?"

Mack looks over his shoulder as he lifts the ladder off the wall. "Put your money away! It's enough that you'll honor the Martinelli name and bring that chest back to its glory."

Rafe slips that wallet back in his pocket. As he does, Mack gets that long ladder through the shed door. He keeps going, too, carrying the ladder around the side of the cottage to the front yard. Rafe follows behind him, stopping nearby when Mack leans the ladder high against the roofline. "Before I climb to those gutters, Rafe, how about I give you a hand moving that blanket chest back inside before the snow falls? You know, since you're here, we'll take care of it together."

Rafe tries to argue, but Mack insists strongly enough that he relents. Rafe does have a surprise for Mack, though, once they cross the street. "The chest's on casters," he says as Mack positions himself to lift it.

"Seriously? So you didn't need me?"

"No lifting necessary." Rafe gives the chest a nudge and it rolls easily along. "I tried to tell you."

"Well, I'll help steer." Standing behind the chest, Mack bends and wheels it up Rafe's driveway. "Hey, guy. Who'd you think would even take your free furniture from this nine-cottage community anyway? Nobody else drives down this dirt road."

Rafe looks over at Mack rolling the chest. "I know, kid. But we just couldn't bring ourselves to ask for your services. Didn't want to bother you," Rafe explains with a shrug. "Looks like this old chest was meant for you to restore, after all. And believe me, Rosa's mighty pleased."

"Good. Now let's get it into your garage for now so it doesn't get snow covered."

It's like they're old pros at this, the way Mack then guides the blanket chest so that its little caster wheels roll along the driveway, and the way Rafe hurries ahead and opens the garage door. Old pros, or old neighbors, anyway.

When they're just about in the garage, Rosa—staying safely distanced—rushes outside from the cottage.

"You didn't take the money, did you, Mack?" she asks.

"Rosa. I couldn't," Mack tells her as he wheels the chest beside Rafe's car. "We're neighbors!"

"Well," Rosa goes on, "you're *going* to take the lasagna, you hear me?"

"The what? The *lasagna*?" Mack repeats.

"No ifs, ands or buts," Rosa insists. "I'm making a lasagna for me and Rafe to have for dinner tonight. I'll make one for you, too."

27

"Rosa," Mack protests. "That's too much."

"Nonsense," she says, and steps closer. Drops her voice, too. Softens it. "*After everything you've been through?*" Her eyes tear up. "I'll just *assemble* the lasagna, okay? You can bake it later in the oven and have a nice, warm dinner."

"Okay, Rosa." Mack tips up his beanie as he turns to leave. "You twisted my arm," he calls over his shoulder, waving to Rafe then, too.

four

ON THE WAY TO HIS cottage, Mack apparently wavers on a decision. It happens when he looks at that crumpled task list, then shoves it—along with his face mask—back in his down-vest pocket. Maybe the promised lasagna sways his decision, too, because he walks straight past his ladder propped to the gutters and goes inside the cottage's sliding door to the kitchen. From the way he looks over at the coffeepot, it's obvious the aroma of the fresh-brewed java gets to him as he deliberates something.

But still, he keeps walking—straight to that sewing room. Straight to a shelf where he lifts off a large work tote. A tote he promptly fills with a staple gun, glue, scissors, roll of foam, and lastly? The bolt of blue fabric veined with gold thread. Then and only then does he check his watch.

"*Already eight o'clock,*" he whispers.

Time enough to fill a thermos with that hot coffee, which he sips while crossing the street back to Rafe's garage. You can't help but see, though, the way he glances once—then again—back at his own cottage's leaf-clogged gutters.

"*After this*," he tells himself while hoisting that heavy work tote higher on his shoulder, "*the gutters*."

So ten minutes and a half-a-thermos-of-coffee later, Rafe moves his car out to the driveway and Mack finds himself bent over a worktable in the back of the garage.

"It's cold, Rafe," Mack tells him while prying off that blanket chest's old seat cushion with a flathead screwdriver. "Go on indoors. Warm up a little."

"Eh. I've got a portable heater out here." He pulls it from a lower cabinet and plugs in the unit. "And the missus is in the kitchen. She already shooed me out once."

"That right?" Mack flips the seat cushion and begins pulling out heavy staples holding the worn fabric in place.

"Yeah. Anyway, we'll be snowed in together after the storm, me and Rosa. So I'll keep *you* company now." Rafe grabs an old beach quilt from a garage shelf. "She takes over the whole kitchen, I'm telling you, when she's making those lasagnas."

Mack pulls the faded green fabric off the bench cushion. "Oh, man, Rafe. Can I ever tell you a story about lasagna."

"Go for it, my friend." As he says it, Rafe opens a webbed chair out in the driveway, sits himself down and drapes that quilt over his lap. "It's nice to have someone to talk to for a change. You know, since the pandemic hit last year, it's harder to connect with people."

"Ain't that the truth."

"Especially when you're my age—livin' the golden years, but higher risk." Rafe shifts in his safely distanced webbed chair. "Now tell me your lasagna saga, why don't you?"

"Okay, then." After replacing the worn-out foam in the cushion, Mack spreads several yards of new blue fabric on Rafe's worktable. "I had quite the lasagna *fiasco* on my first date with Avery last fall." Mack picks up his shears and begins cutting the fabric. "Remember when I told you how we met?"

"Sure. You were picking up her dining room chairs. From her apartment."

"That's right," Mack says while bent over and cutting the blue fabric. "Fall is Martinelli Upholstering's busiest time. *Everyone* wants their homes freshened up for the holidays."

"Yep. And you finagled a dinner date out of her to move her job to the top of the list."

"That I did. And it was on that first date when the lasagna incident happened." Mack sets aside the fabric bolt and wraps the seat cushion with the cut fabric. "And it went something like this."

~

I took Avery to this new Italian restaurant in town, Mack begins. *Heard it was a popular joint. Had a fireplace going on those brisk fall nights. Dim chandeliers. Candles burning. I wanted that atmosphere, because I was really taken with Avery. Problem was, I couldn't be sure if she was as much taken with me. So I had to do everything I could to win her over. You know, like really upping that gentleman ante—picking her up at her place, holding doors open for her, that kind of thing.*

Once at the restaurant, we were seated at a small table right at the window. It looked out onto a scenic spot. There was a wooded area there. And a walking path.

"What a nice place this is," Avery said as I helped slip her jacket off.

"Glad you like it," I answered, sitting across from her. She looked so pretty. Had on a black sweater with a gold bandana-scarf tied around her neck.

We got settled in there. But she surprised me then—before we even looked at our menus. Right away she began digging into her bag and pulled out three fabric swatches. Laid them side by side right there on the table.

"I just can't tell, Mack," Avery began. "Maybe you can help me before we order our dinner."

"Help you?" I leaned my elbows on the table and listened.

"Yes. Which do you think would look better on my dining room chairs?" Carefully, she touched a finger to each sample. There was a plain cream, a navy swirl, and an olive-and-gold tweed. "I pick one," she went on, "then I move the swatch to near the sunlight coming in the window and change my mind. So far, I've narrowed it down to these three."

"Oh, no," I said, sitting back. "You're doing it all wrong."

"But the decorating articles all say—"

I shook my head. "Decorating calls for decisiveness."

"What? But everything I've read says to consider many factors. Lighting, usage. Type of wood, even. Which is cherry."

"I know. So you're talking a formal look."

"Right. But I like my dinners more casual. So there's an inconsistency between use and furniture style."

"Now you see? That would be TMI."

"TMI?" Avery asked.

"Too much information. Gets your decision all muddled up."

To impress her, I was trying to act all confident—because I was actually making some of this up on the fly. So I figured a little bravado wouldn't hurt.

"You can't overthink it," I explained to Avery, picking up each of the three fabric pieces, then spreading them in my hands like three playing cards. "You've got to browse your options—"

"Which I have. Exhaustively."

"That's where you're getting stuck. Just try this."

"I'm listening," Avery said, pulling her chair in closer.

So did I. Pulled in my chair and set those fabric pieces down again, right on the table. "Browse, then right away go with your gut. Or your heart. And whichever fabric appeals to you first?" I said, leaning back now. "That's the one," I added with a clear nod.

Oh, I was the man. I had it going on, guiding Avery in her choice.

Or so I thought.

Because the waiter came around just then, ready to take our

33

orders. Which gave me the perfect opportunity to demonstrate my decisiveness.

"Listen, you can't go wrong if you go with your gut. Like this, Avery." I opened my menu, scanned the selections pretty quickly, dragged my finger down the list and told the waiter, "I'll have the Farm Table Lasagna." With that, I flipped the menu closed and set it aside.

"Are you sure, sir?" the waiter asked me back. "Because generally that meal is intended—"

"Of course I'm sure," I interrupted. "The Farm Table Lasagna sounds amazing. All that organic cheese. And sauce made with native tomatoes. Fresh spinach. Really," I told the waiter standing there with his pen poised over that order pad. "I don't need to see anything else." As I said it, I nudged the closed menu right to the table edge.

"But—" the waiter began.

"No buts," I insisted.

"In that case," the waiter went on. "Would you like to be seated at a more ... comfortable table?"

"What?" I asked. "No. No, this table for two is perfect." I looked out at the evening, where some colonial lampposts were coming on. Then I looked at Avery across from me. "We'll stay right here at the window."

"The thing is, Rafe?" Mack says now while stapling the folded-over corners of the gold-threaded blue fabric. "This waiter was making me look bad. Casting doubt on my decision-making. So I stuck with my choice and nodded for Avery to order."

"I'll have the pasta primavera," she quietly said, looking up from her menu.

34

And all was good. We shuffled around her fabric samples. Set them aside and talked about our jobs, families. The usual. Our salads were delivered. We sipped our wine. She settled on the olive-and-gold tweed for her chairs. And the talk? It came easy. Everything felt right.

But things started to change when Avery's meal was delivered.

"I'm sorry," the waiter told me after setting down her plate. "But the Farm Table Lasagna is taking a little longer. Would you like anything while you wait, sir? Fresh bread, maybe?"

"No, no. I'll save my appetite."

Oh, and I should've been clued in by the way he raised an eyebrow, then. And by the smile he fought. But ... I was distracted by the beautiful woman across from me. Avery nibbled at her food and made small talk while we waited for my lasagna to arrive.

And arrive it did.

Ten minutes later, some of the restaurant staff emerged from the kitchen. They wheeled a food cart in our direction. A food cart covered with my Farm Table Lasagna. The thing is, it filled the entire length of a farm table. Thus ... Farm Table Lasagna. That platter must've been, oh, three feet by two feet— at least! Because it was meant for the banquet room in back. Meant for private events with small crowds. So before they could even serve my lasagna, the staff pushed several small tables against our window bistro table—just to make room for my dinner. I kid you not, it was the largest lasagna I'd ever seen.

"Mack Martinelli!" Avery exclaimed.

She did more, too. She just burst out laughing. And seriously, we both couldn't stop laughing for the rest of the dinner. People strolling the walkway outside the window smiled when they saw our table. Patrons at other tables turned for a look, too. With more smiles, and nods, and waves.

As for me? Hell, I barely made a dent in that lasagna. Or talked about anything else but that lasagna! And I looked like a complete fool, too. I'm sure of it. So much for my confidence.

But Avery, sweet Avery. She never stopped smiling the whole night. Through dinner, through our tiramisu dessert and coffee. The entire time, the couple of hours sitting there in our little Italian restaurant together, was just as fine as that food.

⌒

"And you know something, Rafe?" Mack staples a dust-cover fabric on the back of the now-reupholstered seat cushion. "That night was the first time Avery called me Mack Martinelli like that. No one else really did that, just her. The way she said it so fast? It sounded like one blurred-together word." He pauses his stapling. "*MackMartinelli!*" he rapid-fire whispers then. "Sitting in that restaurant, I pretty much knew," Mack goes on. "Avery was the only woman I ever wanted to say my name like that. And even though that ridiculous lasagna rained on my swagger, it was okay. Because luckily, the whole ordeal led to a second date."

"Did it now?" Rafe asks from his chair in the driveway.

"Yep. Because I needed her help making a dent in the leftovers. And the rest? Well. The rest is history."

Rafe, bundled in his jacket and scarf, sits back in that webbed chair. He squints at Mack and gives a satisfied nod. "Fiasco, indeed! *Really* good to see a smile out of you again," he says.

"Can't help it." Mack spreads furniture glue on the empty top of the blanket chest's lid before pressing the reupholstered cushion securely into place. And he's still smiling. "Whenever I think of that Farm Table Lasagna night, it just gets to me."

"*Yoo-hoo!*" Rosa's voice calls from outside. Moments later, she's standing at the garage entrance. A foil-wrapped pan of lasagna is in her arms; a scarf is bundled around her neck. "I'll just set this here for you, Mack." She puts the lasagna on a shelf right near the garage door.

Mack looks from the finished blanket chest to Rosa and nods. "That is *really* nice of you, Rosa."

"It's the least I can do." Wearing a thick cable-knit sweater over her black pants, she crosses her arms against the cold air.

"Well, listen," Mack says. "Do you two need a hand moving the chest inside?"

"No, we've got it." Rafe stands and motions between him and Rosa. "The two of us will manage. You go put that lasagna in your fridge, why don't you?"

Mack doesn't argue. Instead he drops his staple gun and tools and glue and fabric remnants and thermos back into his work tote—which he hefts up onto his shoulder. He lifts the lasagna tray, too. And somehow,

37

while crossing the street all laden down, he manages to sneak a look at his watch before noticing the ladder still leaning against the front of his cottage. And gives his head a shake.

"*Have to get to those gutters next,*" he says to himself, throwing a cautious glance to the increasingly cloudy sky, too.

five

"MACK MARTINELLI!" A WOMAN'S VOICE calls out. It rings clearly across the cottage kitchen. "Don't tell me you changed the toaster setting!"

Mack is bent in half in front of the open refrigerator as he slides Rosa's lasagna pan onto a shelf. But the voice gets him to look over his shoulder. Not right away, though. Because first? Well. First he smiles as his eyes drop closed. From the relieved look on his face, you can just see the thankful prayer he's thinking. Or feeling. There's some gratitude being expressed at the sound of the woman's scolding words.

Then he looks over at her. Wearing a brown-and-black Fair Isle sweater tunic over black leggings and fuzzy slipper socks, she's standing at the counter across the room. But she's not looking at Mack. Oh, no. Her elbows are resting on the counter as she bends and fusses with the toaster dial.

"I had to throw out two slices of toast already," she's saying while sliding out the toaster's crumb tray and dumping the charred bits and pieces into the trash. "Both slices were nicely burnt, thank you."

Mack just closes the refrigerator and watches her silently.

Which must get to her, because she looks over *her* shoulder at him then. "I tore the burnt toast to pieces and fed them to seagulls in the yard," she says. "So the food didn't go to waste."

"Aw, Avery. I changed the toaster setting for my bagel this morning," Mack tells her as he pulls off his beanie and gloves and drops them on the counter. "It wasn't toasting dark enough."

"You put it up to almost five!" Again, Avery turns to the toaster. She brushes a crumb off the top, then toys again with the round setting dial. "And I had it set right between two-and-a-half and three." She precisely, slowly, spins the dial back. "It's the perfect setting for my toast. So just leave it there. You can pop your bagel down a second time and it'll get darker, okay?"

"Okay, Ave. I'll learn."

"Good. Because I spent yesterday morning fine-tuning my setting through much trial and error."

Still, Mack only watches her as he crosses his arms and leans against the counter near the fridge. He smiles, too. Slightly. Like he just can't help it. You can tell by the way his eyes never really leave her.

Avery's pulling two fresh slices of bread from a wrapped loaf and dropping them in the toaster. "I was surprised to see you here this morning," she says over her shoulder. "You told me to come a day early and you'd meet me this afternoon."

"I know. But my Saturday delivery was cancelled last minute. It was a big overstuffed chair. Customer got nervous about the bad weather. Rescheduled the delivery for next week, after the snowstorm."

"I get it. Hope you don't mind I parked in the garage."

"Yeah, that's fine. It'll save me from digging out two cars."

"So what time did you get here?" As Avery asks, she keeps a cautious eye on her toasting bread.

"Late last night, actually."

"What?" She whips around at Mack's answer. "I didn't even hear you!" Then she squints at him. "Why didn't you come to bed?"

"Didn't want to wake you, so I slept on the couch. Your sleep's been so fitful."

Avery sighs. "It really has. Until today. I slept in until nine-thirty this morning! Nine-*thirty*, Mack Martinelli! Which is *way* too late for me."

"No." Still, Mack watches Avery across the room. "It's good, Avery."

She glances over at him and gives a knowing nod. "Last night? I slept better than I have in months." There's a pause, then. Avery peers into the toaster slots at her still-toasting bread. "I left the bedroom window open a crack, and that salt air? It does something, Mack, I'm telling you. I wish we could bottle it so I could breathe it back home."

"No kidding." Mack walks closer to her now.

"That salt air is like a sweet elixir. I could just feel it soothing me as I breathed last night," she's saying after her toast pops and she sets it on a plate. "My whole body relaxed. My mind rested."

Mack comes up behind her then. He reaches his arms around her waist as she's buttering her first toast slice. And it's like he almost can't believe she's here. Right *here*. You can tell by the way he bends close and nuzzles her neck first, then rubs his whiskered face against her cheek—getting her to laugh.

"What are you up to this morning?" he asks, his voice low near her ear.

Avery spreads butter on her second slice of toast. "While you work on your dad's list," she says, cutting both toast slices in half, "I'll take a walk on the beach. Going to call my mom, too. I want to be sure my parents are all set for the storm."

"Okay." Mack still has his arms wrapped around her. "That'll give me time to tackle Dad's chores."

In his arms, Avery manages to squeeze around and face him then. A half piece of nicely toasted-and-buttered bread is in her hand. "*Here*," she whispers, giving it to him. "Now that's what happens on the *perfect* toaster setting." She lightly kisses his mouth. "So don't you touch it again!"

Mack takes a hefty bite out of her toast, giving her a wink at the same time.

∼

The morning sky seems conflicted.

Snow, or not.

Storm, or not.

Because the clouds that moved in earlier thin out and show streaks of blue sky behind them now. The sun shines between those clouds and drops golden light on the winter-barren land. But that brisk wind off the sea holds on, whistling across the yards and blowing scattered dried leaves.

With his hat and gloves back on, Mack grabs a dusty work bucket from his truck, then climbs the ladder to the cottage gutters. His boots clump on each rung, one after the other after the other. He carries that old bucket, too, which he hooks onto the top of the ladder. Giving the cottage's long gutter a good surveying then, he reaches his gloved hand into it, scoops out some dried leaves and twigs and drops them in his bucket.

"Mack!" an approaching voice calls out. "Have you seen Mica?"

"Mica?" Mack looks down from his ladder perch at Rafe below on the frozen grass. "Your dog?" Mack asks.

"Yeah. I propped open the back door when Rosa and I maneuvered that chest inside—and Mica must've scooted right out. Didn't even notice until now. But the storm's coming, and she'll get afraid. Or lost." Rafe looks out toward the packed-dirt road and the distant forest. "And I don't want to worry Rosa. She's at the grocery store and would rush right back if she knew."

43

Mack gives a last look at his clogged gutters before grabbing his swinging work bucket and descending to the ladder's third rung. "The dog couldn't have gotten far, Rafe. Between you and me, we should be able to find her in no time." Mack looks out toward the beach. "How about if we split up?"

"Okay. Good idea," Rafe says, turning to scan the yards behind him. The scarf around Rafe's neck blows in the chill wind. "I'll check the woods, over there."

"All right." Mack descends the last few ladder rungs before tossing the work bucket in his truck. "And I'll grab some rope from the shed and head to the beach. Avery took a walk there, so I'll look for Mica and check with Avery at the same time."

On the beach, the coldness is biting. Without the buffer of dunes and sloping lawns, that cold lifts right off Long Island Sound. It's the kind of damp cold that goes straight through to your bones.

Avery's taken every precaution against that happening. Walking the beach, she wears a navy knee-length down puffer coat zipped up tight. A thick pom-pom wool cap is pulled low over her blonde hair. Her black leggings are tucked into plaid-topped duck boots. A blue tartan scarf is looped over her coat; mittens are on her hands.

Every precaution taken. Every protection in place.

She walks close to the breaking waves. Ahead of her, a rocky headland juts out into the Sound. Incoming waves splash on the boulders there. Atop that mighty stone embankment, a sprawling shingled house faces the sea.

As Avery walks in that direction, something catches her eye. A motion. You can tell by the way she suddenly turns.

"*Mica!*" she whispers, squinting at a small dog running across the beach. In a moment, Avery breaks out into a slow trot, calling out for the dog. "Come on, girl," she says as the golden-brown dog with fluffy ears scampers past. "Mica!" Avery calls now, giving chase. Her trot turns into a run down that beach. When the little dog spins around and looks at her, Avery slows her step. She bends low, and keeps her voice gentle. "Come on, Mica. Over here, girl," she says.

Mica seems mesmerized by her tone, and when Avery gets close enough, she rushes forward and scoops up the dog in her arms.

And gasps.

Holding the dog close, Avery gasps again. But this gasp is long—and more strained. It's as though she's trying to suck in enough air to fill her lungs. She spins around, too, away from the wind blowing at her face. Bent in half then, she takes panicked steps this way, then that. Still holding the dog, she finally freezes in place and desperately tries to breathe.

"*Avery!*"

Mack stands at the far edge of his lawn, where a sandy path leads through frozen dune grasses. A length of thin rope is looped in his hand. From his vantage point, there's a clear view down to the beach. And to his struggling wife on it.

"*Avery!*" he calls again, this time as he crashes through the path, swatting random blades of wild grasses out of his way. "Avery, what's wrong?" he calls as he emerges onto the sand and keeps running. In moments, he's at her side. "Avery," he evenly says as she struggles to gasp in enough air to breathe. "*Easy, easy,*" he whispers. "You're okay. You'll be okay."

Avery shakes her head. Her face is flushed; her eyes, panicked. With each attempt to breathe, her lungs seem to close up even more.

"No, Avery." Mack stands right in front of her and takes her shoulders in his hands. "Hey, hey," he says as she squeezes her eyes shut. "Look at me."

She does, watching him with barely a nod.

"Loosen up. Relax. You can do it." As he says it, he's running his hands up and down her arms. The little dog is still in her clutches as Avery wheezes and struggles for a breath. "*Come on,*" Mack whispers.

Silent tears wet Avery's cheeks. But she nods and visibly untenses—somewhat. The dog squirms in her loosened grip. Avery's shoulders drop. She still gasps, but more air seems to get through now.

"That's right." Mack puts an arm around her

shoulders and walks her toward a driftwood log washed up near the dune grasses. His voice doesn't stop calming her the whole way. By the time they get to the log, he takes the dog from her. "Rest, Avery," Mack tells her. "Sit with me."

"*Mack*," she whispers while sitting, her voice hoarse. "I … I … ran after Mica," she manages. "And I couldn't catch my breath." As she says it, she begins crying. And again, she struggles. Again, she tips her head up and wheezes.

Mack slips that rope through Mica's collar, then pulls Avery close and presses his mouth to her ear. "You're okay. *Shh. Shh.*" When she eventually quiets, he puts little Mica back in her lap. "Here. Pet the dog. It'll help."

Avery does. Gently, her hand strokes the dog's long, fluffy ears. She strokes Mica's silky back, too, and dips her face to the soft fur. "Mack," Avery says then. "I can't even run after a *dog*. It was just a trot—and I *still* can't breathe right."

"You're getting better, though."

"But sometimes I can't fill my lungs." There's a quiet pause, then, "And I get so afraid."

"I know. But the doctors say you're doing good. It just takes time to recover."

Avery looks out at the beach. The water beyond ripples beneath that stiff, cold breeze. Small waves lap at shore. "When I got winded running after poor Mica, my breath caught. And it felt shallow, *like it did in the hospital*," she whispers, swiping at more tears.

"*Shh*. Come here."

Avery leans into Mack on the log, and he presses a kiss on the side of her face.

"You just panicked, Ave, and that heightened it all. Your doctor said that happens."

The way the two of them sit so close on that log, they seem to be shielding each other from the cold sea breeze, from the dampness. From some fear. Mack cups Avery's mittened hand in his and rubs it. He leans over to look in her eyes as he talks.

Oh, he's doing more, too—it's obvious. Anyone could see he's checking on her well-being. He's being certain her color is okay; her eyes, clear; her breathing, regular.

"The doctor also said it's so important to rest. Which is why I wanted you to come here this weekend, Avery. To get away. To breathe the salt air." Mack pulls off a glove and reaches his hand to her face. He brushes back a windblown strand of hair. Strokes her flushed cheek. "Feel better now?"

Avery only nods. She still holds Mica, too. The little dog's curled up in the warmth of her long parka coat.

"Let's head back?" Mack asks. "I'll walk you home, then drop Mica off at Rafe's before I get to those gutters."

"Okay."

"Maybe take a nap at the cottage. That took a lot out of you just now."

"*I will*," Avery whispers. "But can we just sit here for a minute longer?"

"Of course, sweetheart." Mack touches the furry pom-pom on her wool cap. "Of course."

They don't talk, then. They just sit together, facing the sea.

Waves break.

The cold, salty breeze hitches.

More silvery clouds blow across the sky, obscuring the blue again.

A seagull swoops on an air current.

Avery just breathes.

The world turns.

⁓

Mack quiets while walking back to the cottage. The change is noticeable, though Avery doesn't seem to mind. It's more like she understands. Mack takes Mica, adjusts the dog's rope-leash and sets her on the beach. When they emerge from the sandy path through the dune grasses onto the sloping lawn, Avery walks beside Mack. Their words, though few, are enough. Caring. Worried. They stop on the deck, where Mack checks to be sure Avery is all right now.

Avery pats the dog goodbye, then assures Mack she'll be okay. Assures him, while standing at the back slider, that she's going to have a glass of water and close her eyes for a while. Mack leaves a kiss on her forehead and turns to deliver Mica back to Rafe and Rosa.

~

But by the time he crosses the dirt road and gets to their cottage front door, there's that change again. Mack's knock on the door is more a sharp rap. Over and over and over. When no one promptly answers, he glances around and knocks again, louder this time. At the third intrusive knock, Rafe opens the door.

"Mack." He sees the dog at Mack's feet then. "Mica!" he says as Mack tosses the roped leash down and steps far back. Rafe scoops up the rope and tugs the little golden dog inside.

"She was on the beach," Mack tells Rafe, then turns and gives an agitated wave as he walks away. If you'd call it a wave. Some might think it more a motion saying he's had enough. Saying this morning's gone on *long* enough. Mack trips, too, on some heave in the frozen lawn. But he regains his footing and keeps going, right through a picket-fence gate that doesn't catch behind him. So he bangs it shut once, then again. Harder.

While watching this from his cottage doorway, Rafe unties Mica's rope-leash. He leaves her in the cottage, reaches for a nearby coat, shuts the door and half trots after Mack. "Slow up, there," he calls out while slipping an arm into the wool coat.

"Damn it, Rafe." Mack looks back at him. "You

50

ought to get a legit fence! For God's sake, you've got this huge yard—and all you ever did is put up this flimsy thing?" With each phrase, each word, Mack's voice gets louder. "A picket fence with a *busted* gate that your dog slips through? Come *on*, already," he yells while throwing up a hand toward the open gate.

"I'm telling you," Rafe says while putting his other arm in a coat sleeve and hiking up the wool coat close beneath his chin. "Mica's never gotten out before!"

"Well, you want to make a habit out of it *now*?" Mack tosses back at him while slamming that picket-fence gate shut. Slamming it so hard, anyone watching would expect it to break right off the hinges. "Spend some money and fix your damn gate!" he yells before storming off.

"*Hey!*" Rafe yells back. Then he stops still and waits for Mack to look at him. "What's the matter with you?"

"What's the matter with *me*?" Mack turns and takes a step, just one, toward Rafe.

"Yes!"

Mack takes another step closer. "What would you do if I weren't here, *huh*? Your dog would've been three beaches over by now. Or been lunch for some bobcat in the woods."

"Wait." Rafe turns up his coat collar against the cold. "What would *I* do if you weren't here?"

"That's right." Mack throws up an arm toward Rafe's cottage. "With your lousy fence. Your old blanket chest. Your runaway dog. It's all I can do to keep your place in order."

51

From a safe distance away, Rafe squints at Mack. Drops his voice, too. Drops it low. Serious. "I don't think we're talking about me and Mica anymore, kid."

Mack pulls off his sherpa-lined beanie, drags a hand through his dark hair and looks past Rafe, then straight at him.

"You come around back," Rafe tells him while swinging open that troublesome picket-fence gate. He holds it open, too. "Right *now*."

Mack pulls his beanie back on and just stands there, arms crossed in front of him.

"Rosa's still at SaveRite, stocking up before the storm hits. So I've got some time to talk." He hitches his head toward his backyard before heading that way. "Let's go."

Rafe's patio is buttoned up tight for the winter. Table's covered; chairs are stacked in his shed; autumn's dried leaves, long blown away. So he carries two *kitchen* chairs outside instead and sets them about ten feet apart on that patio. By the time Mack rounds the cottage corner, Rafe's coming outside again. This time, he's holding two long-stemmed, bowl-shaped crystal glasses and a bottle of liquor.

"Let's have a talk, my friend," Rafe says. "Socially distanced, of course." He puts his things on the covered patio tabletop. Carefully then, he fills the two glasses and sets one on the far chair for Mack.

Mack walks over, picks up the odd-shaped glass and swirls the clear liquor in it. "What the hell's this?"

"Grappa. A form of brandy, actually. And it'll bring you back to the Italian old country in one sip." Rafe raises his glass toward Mack, then sits on his own chair facing him.

"Never had grappa before."

"What?" Rafe pulls a tweed newsboy cap out of his coat pocket and puts it on. "With a name like Martinelli?"

"Heard of it. Never drank it." Again, Mack gives his glass a swirl, watching the sloshing liquor as he does.

"You kidding? How old are you?"

"Thirty-four."

"Sheesh. Over three decades and you never even had a sip?"

"Nope. Not until now."

Rafe sits back and takes a long swallow from his glass. "Many Italians, Rosa and myself included, swear by grappa's curative powers. It's been said to treat everything from stomachaches to sadness."

"*Just what the doctor ordered,*" Mack says under his breath. "Well. Here goes," he tells Rafe, then takes a good taste of the liquor. And promptly winces—strongly. And gives a hard shake of his beanie-capped head.

"Grappa's made from what's left over after winemaking—grape seeds, stalks, pulp, stems. Some folks call *this* liquor firewater, Mack."

"Or kerosene. Shit, Rafe. That's potent stuff."

"It's an acquired taste. The more pain you have in life, the more you grow to like it." Rafe takes another swallow of the grappa. "Now, why don't you tell me what's *really* going on with you?"

Mack takes another drink of the liquor, too. Tips his glass up high and manages a hefty swallow. Another wince, too. "It's my wife," he says then.

"Avery?"

Mack nods. "She had an incident on the beach just now. When she was running after your dog."

"*Avery* did?"

"That's right. I was just going through the dune grass to the beach and spotted her when it happened. She was running after Mica—when she suddenly couldn't get a breath."

"Oh my God. She really couldn't breathe?"

"Hardly."

"I'm sorry, Mack. I had no idea."

"It happens, since her hospital stay. And then, making the situation worse, panic set in." Mack pauses, swirling the liquor in his glass. "Whether it's more panic than reality?" Mack turns up a hand. "But it's still very real. Her throat was closing up on her." He stands then, and paces behind his chair. Then sits again. "And it's frustrating, Rafe. Really frustrating. It just doesn't quit, that virus. I mean, Avery's anxiety is amped, and she's still tired from it all. Sometimes just folding the laundry exhausts her."

54

Sitting there on Rafe's kitchen chair, Mack leans forward, sets his arms on his knees and drops his head. And in that posture, and silence, you can read it all. It's all visible. Everything that's been on Mack's mind since Avery caught that virus six months ago. In the slump of his strong shoulders and slight shake of his head, it's all there. Every worry; every lost night of sleep; every moment of anger; every phone call, doctor appointment, temperature check. Relief's there, too. Somewhere in it all.

When Mack raises his head and gives Rafe the litany of worries weighing him down, his body language makes perfect sense. And his voice? It's monotone, as though he's too fatigued to put any energy into the words. Words about the shadows he notices under Avery's eyes in a certain light. Or the weight she's lost, even though she'd only been on a ventilator for days. And the way the whole ordeal robs her of sleep— because sleep reminds her of the darkness she sank into, alone, when intubated. So she's often afraid to even *fall* asleep now, thinking she might not wake up.

"She hates that the most, Rafe. Hates it," Mack admits, his voice low. "Remember how I told you that Avery and I asked each other personal questions last summer?"

Rafe nods. "Favorite food. Biggest fear."

"You got it. And that damn virus nailed her worst one. Fear of the dark, Rafe. That was her fear before she even *got* sick. And then going on the ventilator

55

brought her into the *worst* darkness. Her biggest fear came true. She's even got the scar to prove it."

"Scar?" Rafe asks.

"On the underside of her wrist. It happened when she was sedated. *And* on the ventilator. Apparently, in that state, she struggled to pull out the breathing tube. Resisted it. So the hospital staff had to tie her wrists to the bedframe to prevent her from doing any harm to herself. There's a small scar there now, from her struggles."

"*Jesus*. I had no idea."

Mack takes a long breath, and finishes what's left of his grappa in one long gulp. "Even though it's been six months, Avery's not out of the woods with this, Rafe. Oh, she's had her follow-up medical appointments and done some physical therapy. Had to work on her walking a little bit. Her writing. Her speech. You name it, she's done it. Tackled it. But that godawful virus *still* sneaks up on us sometimes—all these months later. Not often. But it does."

"Like it did today?"

"On the beach."

"Oh, Mack." Rafe leans forward on his chair. The clouds in the sky above are grayer now. "Poor Avery. It breaks my heart to hear all this."

"Mine, too. She's only thirty years old and she had a rough bout."

"If there's *anything* Rosa and I can do, you let us know."

"The thing is? Sometimes even *I* don't know what to do to help her. And I'll never fully know what she's been through—fighting for her life in the ICU. She doesn't talk about it much, just bits and pieces. So I don't push her."

"She'll come around, don't you worry."

A shrug from Mack, then. "It just makes me mad. Mad at something. The world. God. Fate. Mad that my sweet Avery's had to suffer the way she did. She did everything right, took every precaution. Didn't hop on planes or whisk off to hotels for pointless vacations. She didn't get together with friends. Or her parents. Didn't take *any* risks. She went to the God damn post office to pick up our mail after our honeymoon here at the cottage—and that was it. And before, Rafe? Well, *you* caught some of my anger. I'm *really* sorry I snapped at you like that. You didn't deserve it."

Rafe reaches for the bottle of grappa. "All I can say, Mack," he offers while pouring a splash of the liquor in his glass, "is that your anger? It's good. Because it comes from your love for Avery. And that's what'll get you through all this. Trust me."

Mack's quiet for a moment, saying only, "It's a decent thought."

Rafe walks a few feet closer and sets the bottle of liquor down for Mack. When Rafe returns to his seat, Mack stands and gets the bottle. He refills his own glass before sitting on the kitchen chair again.

They don't say much on the patio, then. At one

point, Rafe lifts his glass in a hopeful toast. Mack obliges, lifting his glass, too. When Mack takes a swallow of grappa now, the wincing is gone. The liquor goes down smoother, apparently.

Sitting there, Mack turns up the collar of his down vest while nursing his drink. The sea breeze carries the sound of waves breaking down on the beach.

"Surf's picking up some," Rafe quietly says, "with the storm coming."

A seagull cries, too, over and over and over again.

~

Back in the cottage later, Mack checks on Avery. She's fast asleep in the bedroom. He watches her sleep. And breathe. Easily. There's a patchwork quilt folded on the end of the bed. He lifts the quilt and gently lays it over her resting body.

He does more, too. In the kitchen, he makes two sandwiches—roasted chicken with tomato and shredded lettuce. Some mayo, a little oil. One sandwich he wraps and leaves in the refrigerator. The other he puts on a blue stoneware plate and sets on the kitchen table, where he sits, too. Sits facing the slider and the sloping backyard, all while gauging the cloudy sky outside as he eats lunch. And again, just like in the morning with his bagel, he does nothing else. Doesn't put on the TV. Doesn't read a magazine. Doesn't check his cell phone. He just eats his sandwich. Gets a small bag of potato chips, too. Opens it, starts to reach in for a chip—and then dumps the entire bag beside the sandwich on his plate. And eats. Just eats. Chews, and drinks a glass of seltzer, and pats his mouth with a napkin.

He checks on Avery again, too, before putting on his vest, beanie and gloves.

"*Gutters, gutters,*" he whispers at the same time.

Once outside, Mack grabs that old work bucket out of his pickup truck again. A few gutter leaves from earlier line the bottom of the big pail. But when he spots the pile of snow stakes in the truck bed, he looks around—including another glance at the sky. And puts the bucket back in the truck.

"*Better get those stakes in first,*" he tells himself, lifting a canvas log-tote filled with tall, thin poles. It doesn't take long to line the cottage driveway with them. After spacing out each orange-and-white stake, he inserts them into the ground—lifting his booted foot to the pole's foot brace and pressing firmly. He lines a few on Rafe's driveway, too, before heading down the dirt road into the forest. In spots that don't get much sun, the road is dusted with light snow. The towering tree branches are, too. As Mack walks, there's little wind. That forest provides a barrier against it. And though the sky is cloudy, some midday light drops through the trees' outstretched bare branches to the road. So shadows on the road are pale; the woods, winter still.

There's only the sound of Mack's booted feet crunching on the packed dirt and pressing in the snow stakes around curves here, and there. It's just him in the woods. Mack alone, with trees towering over him. Concealing him. You could look once, then again, and lose sight of the man against the tall tree trunks and shadows. He keeps walking, further and further along the road into the woods until he's out of stakes.

~

When Mack finally emerges, that canvas log-tote is partially filled again. It now holds a couple pieces of firewood and a handful of pinecones he dropped in on the way back. As he approaches his family's one-story shingled cottage, he slows. Slate-blue trim frames the cottage windows. That empty trellis is crisscrossed with the twiggy winter remnants of wild roses.

And those gutters. You can't miss the leaves spilling from them. With a defeated shake of his head, Mack checks his watch, then grabs the ladder lifted to those gutters. He carries that ladder around back to the shed, then walks into the cottage through the kitchen slider.

Avery is still asleep—the quiet cottage clues him in. Mack pauses just inside the door and listens. After a hushed moment, he sets his canvas tote on the kitchen table, pulls off his gloves and hat, and listens again. In the muted silence, he unsnaps his down vest and hangs it on a wall hook, then turns to the oven.

It's obvious now that only one thing is on his mind.

One person.

Avery.

Obvious by how noticeably quiet he's being while setting the oven temperature, and opening flatware drawers and cabinets and the refrigerator.

Quiet as he makes a salad at the counter—rinsing the tomatoes and cucumber and shredded lettuce. Sprinkling cheese and croutons in the filled salad bowls.

Quiet as he slides the foil-covered lasagna pan into the warmed oven.

Quiet still as he finds a linen tablecloth in a built-in cupboard in the dining room. As he moves a wicker basket of seashells from the distressed-white dining room table to a chair. As he carefully spreads that tablecloth over the table, pressing out any wrinkles in the linen.

Quiet as he sets out blue stoneware plates. As he takes wine goblets from that white built-in cupboard and puts the glasses on the table. As he pulls cloth napkins from the cupboard drawer. As he moves that wicker basket of salty seashells back to the center of the dining room table.

Quiet as he first glances down the hallway toward the bedroom, then retrieves the canvas tote from the kitchen counter. The same tote he just carried through the woods.

Quiet still as he pulls the frosty pinecones from that tote and, one by one, nestles them among the seashells—clam and scallop and blue mussel and channeled welk.

six

"YOU DID ALL THIS?" AVERY asks later in the cottage dining room.

Mack looks at her from the head of the table. "All what?"

"Come on," she says sitting near him and sweeping her fork to the beautiful tablescape. Dried hydrangea blossoms spill from a white ceramic pitcher. Beside it, that basket of seashells is dotted with pinecones. Above it all, contrary to the mismatched painted chairs around the table, is a crystal chandelier. Dusty prisms and pendalogues hang from faded brass pins. There are large windows overlooking Long Island Sound, too. The windows fill the wall beside that chandelier. In the light of day, its crystals must catch the blues of the sky and glimmer like sea glass in the white-painted dining room.

But for now? That chandelier shines on one epic Italian dinner.

"I mean, look at this spread," Avery persists,

nodding to the salad bowls and wine and breadbasket. And that lasagna.

"It was nothing," Mack tells her, getting her to wave him off with that fork. A fork she can't keep out of the food.

Neither can he.

Their silverware clicks and clacks on those blue stoneware plates. Forks scoop up pieces of lasagna. Knives are set on plate edges after buttering thick slices of warm bread. There's more fork-jabbing, this time at lettuce and tomato wedges in salad bowls. There's even the muffled sound of wine goblets being set on the linen tablecloth. Tiny cream tassels dangle along its hem.

And they talk.

Avery says how she saw Rafe and Rosa when she arrived yesterday. "After I pulled into the garage, they came over to the yard. Said hello. Chatted a little. I really like them, Mack."

Mack nods, and mentions the approaching snowstorm, and still-clogged gutters.

"You didn't get to them yet?" Avery asks.

Mack shakes his head while eating.

"But they were at the top of your father's list!" As she says it, Avery drags a hunk of bread through tomato sauce on her plate.

"I wanted to get dinner ready. And then it was too dark out. Hopefully I can clear those gutters first thing in the morning, before the snow comes down too heavy."

64

Avery nods, but says nothing. She's too busy eating that tender, sauce-covered lasagna. "It was so nice of Rosa to give us this," Avery says as she lifts a cheesy forkful. "Oh my gosh, it's amazing."

"Really …" Mack, flannel shirt cuffs turned back, eats a mouthful. "Maybe gives your *favorite food*," he says, air-quoting the words, "a run for its money?"

"My mom's meatloaf?" Avery forks off another piece of lasagna and samples it. She leans back and savors the flavor. "Close," she finally says, patting her mouth with her napkin. "But a close *second*."

Mack tips his wineglass to hers. "I figured as much." After sipping his wine, he touches Avery's cheek, then strokes her sandy blonde hair. It hangs long, past her shoulders, and is loosely twisted into a side braid. "You look better now."

Avery nods, and squeezes his hand against her face. "Sleep comes so easy here. I can't believe I napped all afternoon."

"The salt air really must do it."

"There's nothing like it." She gives Mack a questioning smile then.

"What?" Mack asks.

"Can you open the kitchen slider? Just a crack?"

"And let in some of that air? Absolutely."

Mack gets up and does just that. In minutes, the cool air lifting off the salty sea drifts into the cottage. When he returns to the dining room, Mack brings the blue throw from the couch and drapes it on Avery's lap.

65

"Good?" he asks.

"Good," she says. "Perfect, actually."

~

And it is perfect. No one would want to leave that room. Would want to stand and push in their painted chair. Would want to cork the wine bottle and call it a night.

No one, including Mack and Avery—who dine on, and sip on, together in the evening light. Winter twilight presses against the windows. The crystal chandelier glimmers above.

As they're lingering, and sipping, Avery tips her head. "What's that I'm hearing?"

A soft, but complex noise makes its way inside through the open kitchen slider and floats into the dining room. The noise could sound like the chandelier's crystal pendants, clinking in a halting sea breeze. Or it could be a melodic sound of nature, snowy ice crystals maybe, tap-tap-tapping at the frosted windowpanes as a winter storm approaches.

"Remember Mr. Hotchkiss?" Mack asks. "My neighbor?"

"Oh, Mack." Avery spins and squints at the darkness outside. "Is that his piano?"

Mack nods, motioning his half-filled wineglass to the window.

Avery turns back to him. "How could I forget Mr.

Hotchkiss? We danced to his piano playing last summer." Avery looks outside again. "To *Amazing Grace*. We waltzed right on your stone patio that night."

"That's him now," Mack explains. "He's warming up."

"Warming up?"

"He gives a New Year's recital every January. Been at it for twenty years now. Opens up his home to all the neighbors here at Hatchett's Point."

As Mack's talking, Avery stands and goes to the window. She looks out in the direction of Mr. Hotchkiss' cottage.

"They leave the cottage all decorated from Christmas," Mack goes on. "It's pretty grand, actually, seeing their white Christmas tree lit up. And tiny lights and garland strung everywhere. Then there are champagne toasts all around, for everyone to ring in the New Year."

Avery turns toward Mack still sitting at the table. "Must've been kind of sad this year, in the pandemic. You can't do all that. It's too risky."

Mack sits there looking at Avery. "He's giving his recital tonight," he says.

"Tonight?" Avery steps closer to the window and peers out into the dark again. The cottage next door is all illuminated. Windows are aglow. Twinkle lights shine here and there.

Mack joins Avery at the window and looks out with her. "The recital was supposed to be last weekend, but it got rained out," he explains. "Because it was going to be *outside* this year. And since the piano had already been moved to the sunporch for the event? They're trying again today."

"Really?" Avery asks.

"Yeah. Hotchkiss and his son set up spaced-out seating in the yard. Got the firepit all stacked. Cleared the patio if someone wants a dance or two. Even though most folks like to just sit and listen to the music playing."

Avery takes Mack's hand in hers. "That sounds so *nice*, Mack!"

"It always is." Mack touches Avery's side braid. And tips his head. And watches her. "I just didn't know if you'd want to go."

"I'd *love* to go!" Avery turns to the window again, saying over her shoulder, "I feel a lot better now. And it would be so much fun, sitting all cozy outside and hearing that *beautiful* piano playing."

"It's not supposed to start snowing until late." Mack steps behind Avery, wraps his arms around her waist and looks outside over her shoulder. "So ... would you like to make it a date, Mrs. Martinelli?"

"Definitely. We haven't had one of those in a while." She twists around and kisses Mack's cheek, then glances at the same Fair Isle tunic sweater over black leggings that she's had on all day. "But what can I wear?"

"Anything you have is fine, Avery. Everyone's going to have fleece blankets over them, anyway."

Avery spins back toward the window. She cups her face against the glass for a better look at the illuminated cottage in the winter night. "I'll see if I can jazz up an outfit somehow."

～

"Hey, good-looking," Avery says later when Mack walks into the kitchen. "You've gone formal," she adds while slipping into a sleek camel coat—belted at the waist.

"I did." Mack changed his shirt to a black denim button-down. Now he tightens the black-and-gray diagonal-striped necktie added to his look. "Found this in my father's closet here."

"*Very dapper, Mack Martinelli,*" Avery murmurs as she reaches to a chair, lifts his black peacoat off the back and holds it open for him.

Mack slips it on and buttons up the double-breasted coat. His formal necktie is visible in the open collar. When he turns to Avery in her wool coat and shearling-lined suede boots over brown velour leggings, he smiles with a shake of his head. You might think he just can't believe she's actually here. That she's a vision. "And you, Mrs. Martinelli," he manages, "look beautiful."

"Oh, wait! I forgot something." Avery hurries down the hall, returning moments later with what looks like a fabric remnant from the sewing room. It's a plush leopard-print fabric, with its uneven texture giving it

69

the look of real fur. She takes the long, wide piece of fabric, knots it just so, then loops it around and around her shoulders and neck, over her camel coat. The wrap looks almost like a winter shawl now, the way she casually drapes it. After skimming her fingers over her piecey side braid, she lifts the rear folds of her pseudo leopard-shawl right over her head like a loose cape.

Mack puts on his wool beanie. He steps closer, too. Extends his arm and takes Avery's hand in his, giving her a slow twirl before they head out.

The night turns magical then.

It's as if Mother Nature gently opens her arms and sprinkles down snow-dust from the cloudy skies. The snow flurry is just enough to create that wondrous atmosphere—casting a spell on the beach neighbors gathered in Mr. Hotchkiss' backyard. Large spray-chalk circles have been outlined on the grass, keeping the couples and small families appropriately distanced during this pandemic performance. *Welcome* signs indicate that each circle is designated one per cottage, and to find the circle with your street number on it. In the firepit, flames crackle and snap, making a nice warming station for cold guests. Painted signs mounted on a nearby tree request that only one couple at a time dance on the patio, near the birdbath, and on the gazebo. Each folding chair comes with a fleece blanket.

And tiki torches outline the dark yard, throwing wavering light on the guests.

Then there's the cottage. Paned windows softly glow. Twinkle lights glimmer on a tall white Christmas tree. Swags of balsam garland loop around the deck railing. Deck posts are tied in blue velvet bows. Candlelit lanterns are scattered here and there.

But all of that pales beside the sunporch.

A wall of paned windows—an entire wall—faces the yard. Each window is open to the night. On the other side of those windows is Mr. Hotchkiss' piano. Candles—tapers and votives and pillars—flicker atop it. On the far wall, a roaring fire burns in a floor-to-ceiling stone fireplace.

Guests continue to arrive in the tiki-torch-lit yard. Everyone's dressed in their finest attire—warm wool coats and fluffy earmuffs; sparkling capes and elbow-length gloves; rhinestone hairpins and furry trapper hats. On their way to their respective circles, people wave at familiar faces. Neighbors chat from a distance, and nibble on treats from individual bakery boxes filled with fudge brownies and raspberry Danish and crumb cake. Some guests walk across the yard for a glimpse at Long Island Sound beyond.

Until suddenly—silence.

It's a silence that comes when every cottage window, except on the sunporch, goes dark.

It's a silence that gets everyone to sit in their chalked circle and watch that cottage sunroom. When they do,

71

Mr. Hotchkiss takes his seat at the piano. He's illuminated by only the several candles atop it, and the roaring fireplace beyond.

The piano, though, is situated in such a way to give the guests a side view. So Mr. Hotchkiss is clearly visible as he takes a long breath. And looks back when a younger man walks into the room and stands beside him. He's tall and lanky, like Mr. Hotchkiss. With a hand on the older man's shoulder, the younger man leans down and says something to him, then walks out through a side door, onto the patio. There, at a microphone stand, he welcomes the guests.

"This year, especially, we're *so* glad you all made it here tonight. And now, for your listening pleasure, it is my *distinct* honor to introduce my father, Mr. Phil Hotchkiss."

As he says the name, Mr. Hotchkiss, dressed in a formal suit and tie, briefly stands and waves hello. When he sits again, he lifts his hands to the keys.

"Take it away, Pop," his son says into the mic.

And when the first notes rise into the night, well you'd be surprised to find a dry eye in the crowd. Strains of *Auld Lang Syne* open the recital, with the piano seeming to be singing a lonely solo as the melody winds outside through the open windows. People lean close. Gloved hands reach out and hold the hands of nearby loved ones. Heads rest on shoulders.

Yes, it's that type of night. One of quiet togetherness. Of neighbors joined by song in this tucked-away beach community. Of Mr. Hotchkiss being the conductor of their hearts as his repertoire works through old familiar standards. There are songs of love, and hope, and sadness. Piano melodies float among the lightly falling snowflakes. And though the Christmas holiday has passed, tonight it doesn't feel so. Especially when Mr. Hotchkiss plays a long Christmas medley celebrating the joy, and solemnity, of life itself.

"Dance with me?" Mack asks upon hearing the first notes of *O Holy Night*. He stands and takes Avery's hand.

Avery stands, too, in her long camel coat. "*But Mack,*" she whispers, leaning close. "*We'll be the only ones dancing.*"

Mack adjusts the loose shawl fabric around her shoulders, her head. "*Come on,*" he whispers back, his mouth pressed to her ear. He tugs her then, gently, toward the patio. "*Be wild.*"

Avery smiles, and in her well-scarved coat, walks into Mack's open arms on the patio. Lantern light casts a glow on them as they press close, and sway, and slowly spin. The lightest snowflakes tumble from the sky. As Mack and Avery dance alone, Mack hums a few bars of the song. The thing is? Anyone watching might see his eyes tear up at certain times. At certain lines about the stars brightly shining.

As though maybe these past months, Mack did look up at the stars. Looked up and maybe pleaded to them.

"*Fall ... on your knees*," he softly sings then, his face close to Avery's. But his breath catches on what could be grief—or gratitude. It's hard to tell. But it's as though Mack maybe *has* fallen on his knees. As though he maybe knows *exactly* what that feels like.

"*O hear ... the angel voices*," his singing continues, low and soft, but raspy now.

As though he *did*, one summer day maybe, hear an angel's voice when his Avery was finally wheeled out of the hospital and safely returned to him. Heard the angel's voice when, sitting in her wheelchair, Avery reached for him and said his name.

In person.

Face-to-face again.

"*A thrill of hope ... the weary world rejoices*," he only whisper-sings this time around, then sings no more. Nothing. Not a line, not a word. Not so much as a hum.

Instead, he holds Avery even closer this cold winter night. Smiles when her mittened fingers brush a tear from his cheek. Takes that mittened hand in his and kisses it, then holds her hand between their bodies, his other arm around her shoulders as their dance goes on.

~

After the recital, after the neighbors wave goodbye and call out New Year's wishes, and after Mack and Avery walk across the frosty, snow-dusted lawn to their own cottage and hang up their coats and take off a leopard-print shawl and black-and-gray striped necktie, and put on flannel pajamas and sip hot chocolate and reminisce already about the piano recital—they finally go to bed.

In the bedroom, the blinds aren't drawn on one of the windows—the one facing the distant sea. Snow lightly falls, the white flakes speckling the glass pane. Mack tosses back the blanket and crosses the room, then opens that window an inch or two. When he returns to the bed, he lies on his back and slips his arm around Avery beside him. In the silence, you'd think they're maybe still listening for any lingering strains of that piano.

"*Mack*," Avery whispers.

"What is it?"

Nothing, then. Nothing except quiet—broken only by the hiss of snowflakes tapping at the window. Nothing, until Avery goes on.

"Six months have gone by," she says.

Mack still just lies there, unmoving.

"Six months since I was so sick," she continues. She turns on her side to face him in the dark. Her hand rests on his chest. "And you never left my side, once I came home again."

Mack gives her hand a squeeze. But he says nothing. There's only the darkness in the bedroom. Only the cold night pressing at the window.

"*Thank you*," Avery finally whispers, her voice as soft

as the snowflakes gently falling. She wears a flannel black-and-white buffalo-plaid nightshirt. Matching chenille fuzzy socks are on her feet. Beneath the blankets then, she entwines her legs with Mack's, drawing her soft socks around his ankles. In the dark. Pressing closer to him. Smiling.

A smile he must feel when he bends his head to hers and silently kisses her. His hands cradle her face; his own smile comes then, too. Especially when Avery swings a leg over him and sits on his hips. And runs her hands up and down his arms. And bends low, her blonde hair falling forward as she kisses his jaw. His neck. His shoulder.

"You're pretty cute in that nightshirt," Mack says, squinting through the shadows at her.

"You like it?" Avery asks as she sits up and tucks her hair behind an ear.

"I do. But … come here."

Avery bends a little.

"Closer."

She smiles and, still straddling Mack, brings her face closer to his.

"The thing is," Mack says. "Yeah … I really like this nightshirt. It's very soft." His fingers run across the buffalo-checked fabric at her hips. "*But*," he whispers then, his hands moving to the nightshirt's buttons. "*I think I'll like it better off.*"

Avery joins him in unbuttoning the flannel nightshirt. "*Me, too.*"

When it's unbuttoned, Mack opens the front and runs his hands up her sides, over her breasts, then holds a loose fistful of the open nightshirt in each hand. And tugs Avery closer. So she bends low again, and between kisses, and with her silky hair touching his shoulders, she manages to lift Mack's thermal-weave top off over his head. After she does, Mack sits up on the bed and presses that nightshirt off her shoulders. He does more, at the same time. He leaves light kisses across Avery's shoulders, on her neck, down her bare back.

Until Avery turns to him in the dark. They sit there, facing each other on the mattress. The sheets and blankets are gathered around them. Her nightshirt is tossed aside. Her fuzzy socks are on her feet.

"Let's just stay here forever, Mack Martinelli." Avery glances toward that open window where a cold sea breeze blows. "In our cottage by the sea."

"Well," Mack answers as he lays her down, pulls the blankets up over them, and lies beside her. Beneath those blankets, Avery's hands reach for his flannel pajama bottoms and tug at the drawstring. "We'll stay at least for the night, anyway?" Mack asks, his arm crooked beneath his head as he watches her.

In the darkness, Avery nods. Silently nods against the pillow beneath her head. Tears come to her eyes, just a little. Just for a moment. Just until Mack kisses them away, then feels every curve of her body—his hands touching here, there. Slowly. She reaches for him, too. Their touches are fluid, moving along her hips, up her thigh; down his chest, across his belly, beneath those flannel pants she slides off now.

Those touches come with murmurs, too, in the night. Murmurs that grow quieter as their kisses grow longer. Kisses that grow more urgent as they move together in the shadowy room, beneath the cover of sheets and blankets and the night's darkness.

As snowflakes and cold salt air press in through that open window.

As Mack whispers that he loves her, his voice low.

As Avery holds onto him, maybe tighter than she has in the past.

seven

AN AROMA WAFTS THROUGH THE cottage the next morning. A sweet aroma.

You can tell by the way Avery lies asleep in bed. By the way she turns, and deeply inhales through her nose. Once, then again. Wearing her black-and-white buffalo-plaid nightshirt, she sits up—as though that aroma is pulling her awake. She opens her eyes, too. And runs a hand through her sleep-mussed hair. And gasps when she looks toward the window edged with fluffy snow.

"Mack!" she calls out. "It's *really* snowing now! Did you do the gutters yet?"

From somewhere out in the cottage, his voice calls back. "No. Remember? I told you yesterday I put out the snow stakes instead."

"But those gutters were at the top of your father's list." Avery looks toward that window, where snow falls steady on the other side of it. "You were going to clean them early. *Today.* Those gutters should've been a priority!"

79

Carrying a breakfast tray, Mack comes into the bedroom. "I had other priorities," he says. "Like this."

Avery smiles and fluffs her pillow behind her.

"Perfectly golden toast, Mrs. Martinelli." Mack walks over to the bed. "Cinnamon toast."

"And it smells divine." She props her pillow against the headboard and leans back on it. As she does, Mack sits beside her with the tray. Right away, Avery reaches for a piece of buttered toast and bites in. Her eyes drop closed with the flavor.

"Good?" Mack quietly asks.

"*Just right*," Avery murmurs. She lifts a glass of orange juice off the tray and takes a long sip. *And* scrunches up her nose.

"What's wrong?"

"Mack Martinelli! Don't you know the proper way to serve orange juice?"

Mack gives a short laugh. "Well, I'm sure you're about to inform me," he says, turning her face to his and leaving a light kiss on her lips.

"Wait." Avery pulls back—toast in one hand, orange juice in the other. "And listen. You have to *really* shake the carton first. Put your *soul* into it, you know? Begin the morning with a good ... shake. Because orange juice should be drunk ... frothy." She takes another sip. "It's the best way to start the day."

Mack tips his head. Then reaches for her orange juice glass, which he puts back on the tray. Reaches for her half-eaten toast, too, and sets that on the tray—

after which he slides it all onto the nightstand. "Frothy orange juice is the *best* way to start the day?" he asks.

Avery nods. With conviction. And touches Mack's dark, wavy hair when he moves close.

"*Oh, I can think of another way,*" Mack is whispering to her. She lightly swats his arm, but scoots lower in the bed, too, all while his hands reach beneath that buffalo-plaid nightshirt.

⁓

It seems there's one thing Mack's learned in the past day: Reset the toaster *anytime* you change the setting.

Which he does an hour later, toasting a bagel at the perfect number *five* setting. But he resets the toaster dial right away, then sits at the kitchen table and wolfs down his cream-cheese-slathered bagel. Wasting not a minute, he takes a quick shower then, putting on a pair of black jeans and a heavy sweater afterward. Next up? He pulls on his sherpa-lined beanie, gloves, snow boots and a trail-style parka before heading out. The snow's coming down hard as he treks to the front yard, where he shields his eyes and looks up at those snow-and-leaf-clogged gutters.

Problem is, when he goes into the shed for a hand shovel to scoop out those gutters, he's sidelined by two enormous snow tubes. He grabs his cell phone from his parka pocket and texts Avery. *Meet me out back. Bundle up.*

She replies with, *Blow-drying my hair. Be there in a few.*

Which gives Mack enough time to clear the walkways and a narrow path to the front yard—and gutters. The snow's really falling now, so he almost misses Avery approaching. That is, until she lands a snowball square on his back.

"Hey!" he says, leaning on his snow shovel. "Close your eyes."

"What?" Avery asks in her pom-pom hat and long puffer coat over plaid duck boots.

"You heard me."

"But … don't you want me to help? I could use the electric shovel on the deck—"

"Nope. I want you to have some fun. So close your eyes," Mack repeats.

Avery does. But she warns him, too. "You *have* to clear the gutters, Mack. That snow will freeze and back up onto the roof. And the deck's covered now, too. And the driveway."

"Later," Mack says, heading toward the shed now, snow shovel in hand.

"Can I open my eyes?"

"Not yet." He walks back to her in the yard and holds out one of two snow tubes. "Okay. Now."

"Mack! Where'd you get these?"

"That community cabin I showed you this summer," Mack says as he leads Avery to the sloping backyard. "The one tucked in the woods, just off the road?"

"Sure, I remember." With a blue-and-white tube in hand, Avery sloshes through the fresh-fallen snow.

"That little cabin's stocked with seasonal things for anyone at Hatchett's Point. You know, a few fishing poles. A beach umbrella. Snow tubes—which I grabbed first thing this morning before anyone else did. Come on!" Mack calls, running through the snow ahead of her. "We have the *best* tubing hill here. My parents brought me and my brother here *every* winter, just to tube."

⌒

And so *they* do now, too. They tube.

Avery goes first, after Mack gives her a push down the gentle sloping hill to the snow-dusted dune grasses far below. She spins and wavers this way, then that, across the vast yard. Plumes of powdery snow fan out behind her. Mack gives himself a running start next and follows behind on his own tube—face first, flat on his stomach—whooping and hollering as the snow falls around him.

By the time he meets Avery at the bottom of the hill, she's tumbled out of her tube and is making a snow angel, right there near the dune grasses. Her arms and legs press out the shape of the angel; snowflakes coat her eyelashes. Mack leans over from his tube and gives her a snow kiss. They laugh. He helps her up from the snow, brushes off her jacket, swats at her snowy backside. She tosses another snowball at him. Holding both her hands, he spins her in the snow, getting her to tip her head up and laugh even more, snowflakes dusting her face.

But when she starts to pull her tube back up the long, snowy hill, Mack stops her.

"Oh, no. The Martinellis offer express hill service." As he says it, he unknots the rope looped through her tube handle, helps her sit on the tube, and gives her a hitched pull all the way up the sloping hill.

"You go inside and get warm," he tells her back at the cottage. "I'll bring the tubes back to the cabin for other folks. And I'll get to the gutters now, too."

Avery brushes snow from his face before stamping off her boots on the deck and going inside. "I'll make us an early lunch," she calls out before closing the slider behind her.

Mack waves, then heads around the cottage. He's got the tubes in tow as he clomps through several inches of snow. Walking just past the forest outskirts, he turns into a stand of trees toward that community cabin. It's more of a hut, really, pieced together by the men here with fallen timber and planks of old barnwood. Every summer, it seems someone patches up that cabin, and it gets the job done. Now Mack grabs two fireplace logs from the stack there and heads out of the forest, back to his cottage. On the way, he looks from the snow-laden cottage gutters to his watch, and from his watch to the snow-covered deck and driveway. Stopping in the shed, he grabs the shovel and begins clearing the driveway first, lifting one shovelful after the other and tossing the snow aside.

~

Once the driveway is relatively passable, Avery calls Mack in for lunch. The snow's still coming down, even as the day goes on. They sit at the distressed-white dining room table and eat turkey club sandwiches, split a sliced apple and watch the snow fall outside the windows.

"Did you get the gutters done?" Avery asks.

Mack pushes up his sweater sleeves and sits back in his chair. "Been meaning to, anyway."

"Mack! It's getting late and we have to go soon. I have a video-conference call tomorrow for the new window displays. It's a team meeting, and I'm leading this one."

Sitting forward now, elbows on the table, Mack looks across at Avery. She wears a loose Shaker-knit burgundy sweater over skinny jeans. Her cheeks are flushed from the morning's snow romp; her blonde hair is down. When she tucks it back, her fingers brush across a turquoise stud earring. "Tell me about your new window displays," he says.

"What? Now?"

Mack nods.

And listens.

And watches Avery talk about how each shop window will be decorated like a paned window in the same house. The cookware store will have a kitchen scene. The home goods store? A living room scene, with cozy pillows and throws. The boutique? A walk-in closet scene filled with hung clothes.

"And the mannequins will all be the same family in the house. And there'll be battery-operated candles or lanterns in each window, for a stay-safe, hope-at-home feel at Windmill Plaza."

"Okay." Mack sits back again, this time with a quick breath. "So you'll be busy. Just let me square away these cartons before we get going." He motions to several boxes he'd brought in Friday night, when he arrived at the cottage.

"What's in them, anyway?" Avery asks, twisting around in her chair. "I noticed those boxes earlier."

Mack doesn't tell her. But he shows her, one by one, when he deposits them on the dining room table and tells her to open them.

And so, one by one, she pulls out a new fluffy robe. And soft bootie-slippers. And new thermal pajamas.

"Mack?" she asks, dropping her hands holding a snowflake-striped pajama top onto the table.

"Open the next one."

Avery does, and pulls out a cocoa kit, and the *Mr.* and *Mrs.* coffee mugs they'd received as a wedding gift. "*What is all this?*" she whispers.

"It's for you." Mack moves to a chair near hers and

slides it even closer. And takes her hands in his. "Listen. I've never seen you more rested—and happy—than when you're here at the cottage. All those day trips we took here in the fall? You'd just doze in the warm sun. The salt air."

Avery nods, her eyes moist. "Are you saying what I think you're saying?"

"I hope so. We can stay here for a while. At the beach cottage. For the month of January, at least. Because I want you to *breathe* that salt air. To get *stronger*. Take winter walks in the woods. Have cocoa in the cottage, by the fire."

"Mack Martinelli! Are you serious?"

"I am. I cleared it with the family, and everyone's on board."

"What about work?"

"I'll commute. And check on the house, pick up our mail. The drive's nothing for me."

"But what about *my* work?"

Mack nudges the next box her way. It's filled with her laptop, and journals, and pages of window-display sketches with a handful of colored pencils. "You've been working remotely during this whole pandemic. And you can work from here, too. We've got Wi-Fi. So I brought all cozy things for you, and hope you'll stay here *with* me." He leans close and kisses her. "What do you say, Mrs. Martinelli?"

"Oh my gosh, Mack—yes! I can't believe this!" She swipes at her moist eyes. And scoots into his lap.

Giving him a hug, she whispers near his ear, "*So we don't have to go home today?*"

"No, Ave. I even packed enough clothes. Your favorite sweaters, jeans. So you can settle in here."

With her arms still wrapped around him, she points over his shoulder to the floor. "What's in that last box?"

"Open it."

Avery gets up, crouches to it and lifts the box flaps. "The flannel sheets you got me for Christmas!"

"And a new down comforter. So there's only one thing left for you to do today."

"Which is?"

"Help me make the bed?"

~

They do make that bed.

Kind of.

Between Avery pressing a soft flannel pillowcase to her face, and Mack stripping off the old, thin summer sheets. And Avery wrapping herself in flannel. And Mack flipping open a flannel sheet high over the bed. And Avery sneaking beneath that cozy sheet before it hits the mattress, then motioning for Mack to join her there. And between those soft sheets getting tangled up with lifted-off sweaters and slipped-off jeans and, well, it takes a while.

But eventually, those flannel sheets do get tucked

and the down comforter straightened, and the bed—in due time—gets nicely made.

~

"I'll wash the dishes," Avery says after dinner later that Sunday. "Why don't you check on those gutters now? Sweep away some of the snow there at least?"

Mack's sitting on a kitchen chair and lacing up his snow boots. "Okay, I'll see what I can do."

"And I'll put on a pot of decaf so you can warm up later."

"Sounds good, Avery." Mack pushes in his chair and stomps his boots in place. "We'll make it a couch date."

In no time, he goes through the whole rigmarole— putting on hat, gloves and fleece-lined parka—before trekking to the shed. "*Hand shovel, hand shovel,*" he whispers, searching dusty garden shelves.

And he might've found that shovel, if it weren't for the sand chairs and beach umbrella hanging on the wall by those shelves. He rolls his neck from side to side. Takes a deep breath, and does it. He reaches into his parka pocket for his cell phone. Finds the *Honeymoon Album* in his photos tab. And looks from the chairs hanging on the shed wall now, to the photographs of those same chairs set up on the beach one June night last year.

Quickly, he pockets his phone, lifts the two sand chairs off their wall hooks, grabs the beach umbrella, too, and rushes out the shed door. *"Gutters be damned,"* he tells himself, shaking a loose fist at the falling snowflakes. As he crosses the backyard with all that gear in tow, Mack tells himself one more thing while hoisting up the slipping umbrella.

"If the lights are still on it, even better."

⁓

Even after tubing earlier, it didn't take long for the sloping backyard behind the cottage to be covered with a pristine blanket of new snow.

Pristine, until Mack taps on the kitchen slider and asks Avery to join him outside for an evening snow walk.

Now, two sets of footprints cross that snowy yard.

Mack and Avery, with a blanket and thermos of coffee packed in a tote, head toward the beach path in the distant dune grasses. He reaches a gloved hand to Avery's mittened hand when they walk through the path. Avery's wool pom-pom hat is tugged low against the wintry sea breeze. Her parka is zipped up tight. Cold snow crunches beneath their boots. Long dune grasses droop beneath the snow lining each blade.

As they near the end of the winding path, Avery turns to Mack. "I love snow walks, Mack. Especially at night. But what about the gutters?"

"I'll get to them later. Because first? This." He motions to the dark beach spread out before them now. The sand is snow covered. The waves of the sea look frosty beneath even more falling snow. A light wind blows, swirling the flakes before them. "Someone once told me they found they *liked* sitting on sand chairs," Mack continues as they step onto the beach.

"What are you up to?" Avery asks.

"What am I up to?" Mack points toward the now snow-packed headland jutting out into the water. The sprawling shingled cottage there is capped with snow, too. But smoke curls from its chimney, and lamplight shines in frosted windows.

"It looks so cozy, Mack," Avery says. "Maybe we can have a fire in the fireplace, too?"

"You bet. But you're looking right past my surprise." With that, Mack takes a few steps, then motions to the beach area before that rocky peninsula.

"Just like on our honeymoon!" Avery hurries toward two faded blue chairs set beside a closed beach umbrella. "You put out the sand chairs?" she calls over her shoulder.

"Nope."

Avery stops and spins around to him. "No?"

Mack nods to the chairs while walking closer. "Those there are *snow* chairs," he insists.

"Snow chairs?" She looks from the chairs, to Mack. "What's the difference?"

"Well, I'll tell you." As they walk, there's a lull in the snowstorm. The wind lets up some, and snowflakes

91

tumble from the night sky now. "In a snow chair," Mack begins, "you sit there on a frozen beach where life's gone still. It's blanketed beneath snow. The sand, and sea glass, and seaweed. It's all there, but you can't see it. You just have to … believe. To sit and believe." The way he says it? You could almost get the feeling that Mack once did just that. Sat in a chair in his cottage, with a light on in the window, maybe. Sat alone there and tried to believe Avery would pull through. He stops beside the open sand chairs now. "It's a powerful feeling."

"To believe?"

Mack only nods, and motions for Avery to have a seat. As she does, he unhooks the strap around the closed umbrella.

"We don't need the umbrella up, Mack," Avery tells him. "It's nighttime."

Still, Mack lifts open the umbrella top. When it snaps into place, he flicks on the battery-operated fairy lights entwined on the umbrella's spokes since last June. "Maybe there's no sun, but the umbrella keeps *snowflakes* away, too."

He sits beside Avery then, beneath the twinkling umbrella. They sip coffee from the thermos and don't say too much. Their words are few. But if you were watching, you might think that they *are* doing something as they sit there, sort of quiet. As they face the winter sea splashing cold waves onto the snowy shore. By the way they sit close, and lean in, and sneak light kisses on the barren beach, it's obvious what they're doing is this: Believing.

~

"Have I ever told you how much I love you?" Avery asks minutes later, burrowed beneath the blanket on her sand chair.

Mack only looks at her, leans over and kisses the side of her head. Pats the pom-pom on her winter hat, too. "Look at that cottage," he says, pointing to the snowcapped cottage atop the nearby mighty stone embankment. "It's facing all the elements of the sea and the wind up there. I like to think of it as the fortress of Hatchett's Point."

"Especially the way that peninsula is raised on massive boulders," Avery muses. "It's like the cottage is as strong as the earth it sits upon." She sighs, then. A long, subtle sigh.

"What's the matter?"

Avery looks at Mack. "Nothing. I'm just thinking of a certain day when we were here last June. But it's hard to imagine it right now."

"Imagine summer?"

"Not summer, really. But that actual day when we floated out in our tubes. You led me to the water in front of the peninsula so I could see all the graffiti on the rocks there, from the sea."

"I remember."

"I really loved that day, Mack. Loved seeing all the painted pictures and messages left on the rocks over the years. But sitting here in our winter gear now? Not smelling suntan lotion. Not feeling the sun on our backs. Not hearing the seagulls cry. It's hard to picture floating out there with you."

They're quiet for a few long moments. There's only the winter waves breaking in a silver froth on the snowy beach. And snowflakes falling down from the night sky. Quiet until Avery's voice reaches Mack again.

"But I *did* picture that beautiful summer day. I pictured it on a very dark day, Mack."

Mack says nothing. Instead he reaches over and holds her mittened hand.

"I never told you this. But you need to know," Avery says. "It was after the doctors decided I had to be intubated. Everything happened so fast, once that decision was made. They quickly prepped me to go on the ventilator that day."

"*Avery*," Mack says, his voice low. "Don't put yourself through that again."

"No, it's okay. And it's important you know."

"Know what?"

"Well. You already know my biggest fear."

Mack nods. "The dark."

When Avery answers, her voice is serious. "And it came true, that fear. When I was about to go on the ventilator, I knew. I knew I was headed into the *worst* darkness. And the anesthesiologist saw how afraid I

94

was. He reassured me, and told me I'd be okay." Avery closes her eyes now, as though back in that moment. "Before he administered the anesthesia, he said, *Count with me now. One ... two ...*" Avery opens her eyes and turns to Mack beside her. "But Mack? I remember. I didn't count. I was having such a hard time breathing. God, I was so scared. *And ...* you weren't there. I was alone. I felt myself drifting away, drifting away, and I didn't know if it was the anesthesia ... or if I was dying. So I had to mentally put myself somewhere else." She gives Mack a sad smile. "*Do you know where I went?*" she whispers.

"No."

Avery gives his gloved hand a squeeze. "*Right here,*" she still whispers. "I summoned the feeling of floating on the tubes with you last summer—when we paddled out to the painted boulders. Remember?"

Mack just nods.

"So that's what I tried to do that day in the hospital," she goes on. "I tried to summon the feeling of the sea beneath me. I didn't have long before I'd be unconscious. I knew the drugs were taking effect. But I tried to stay afloat." Avery quiets now, and looks out at the sea. "*To stay alive.*"

Mack follows her gaze. The water is nearly black beneath the snow clouds. Whitecaps edge some of the waves on the stormy evening. "I came here after you were intubated."

"What?" Avery looks to him now. "You did?"

"Yeah." Mack runs a hand along his jaw. "I sensed you more, here. Especially after spending our honeymoon week in this place." He motions to the sea, the beach. "I didn't fully know who you were—until that week. Until you really opened up to me."

"Oh, Mack."

"So when you were on the ventilator, I packed a bag and came here. To the beach cottage. And I put that lamp on in the window for you. Every night. Funny thing is? Then everybody did. It just happened. One by one. No explanation. Starting with that cottage there." He nods to the illuminated cottage atop the boulder-edged peninsula. "Left a single light on all night, in the darkness. Then every cottage followed. And they kept doing that until I let them know you were coming home again. But until then?" Mack hesitates, and shakes his head. A cold wind blows off the water, bringing more snowflakes with it. "They all lit the way back for you," he says, his voice nearly lost in the winter breeze.

～

They don't stay on the beach very long. Nightfall brings a different kind of cold. As Mack closes the umbrella, straps it over his shoulder and hoists the two sand chairs, Avery stands at the water's edge. She wraps the blanket tight around herself. It's hard to imagine what either is thinking.

Or feeling.

Or missing.

Hoping for.

"Ready, Avery?" Mack calls.

She turns to him, and in the darkness, they head back to the beach cottage.

eight

The Following Week

THE SNOW DOES EVENTUALLY STOP falling. But not before nearly a foot of it blankets the beach cottage. And okay, so maybe Mack and Avery take another secret snow day or two in their cozy hideaway, beneath all that snow.

Maybe they steal some time back from the frightening days they'd lost six months ago.

Maybe only smoke curls from the chimney, and lamplight glows in the windows as they cook, and nap, and look out the frosty windowpanes, and drink hot chocolate—sometimes nipped with a shot of wine. They piece together a jigsaw puzzle on that distressed-white dining room table, too. Sink each other's *Battleships* there. And *Scrabble* a day away.

With all that happening, those gutters never do get cleaned out that first snowy weekend.

But neither of them really care. It just doesn't seem to matter.

Oh, Mack Martinelli eventually gets around to them—the best he can. Dressed in his hat and gloves and vest and boots, he props that ladder solid against the cottage. No efforts are spared now. He chips at the frozen snow-pack in those gutters, and brushes away loosened chunks of icy leaves. Finds an errant squirrel's acorn stash, and some seagull feathers, too, blown in by the wind off the sea. Mack keeps at it, from one day to the next. He chisels out and tosses winter debris into that old work bucket hanging from the ladder's top rung.

Problem is, he's a little too late because a water stain has already taken hold on the living room ceiling. Though Mack does more snow-chipping in those gutters every day—sometimes after work—he can't stop that water stain from growing a bit more, too, every day. Finally, in the center of that stain, a little leak comes and drip-drips into a cooking pot Avery sets on the floor beneath it.

Pot or not, some things can't be beat, though. Like nature. At night, beneath the clear, starlit skies over the salty sea, the temperatures drop low. Frigid, some folks would call it. Fit for neither man nor beast. And any snow accumulated on the roof freezes up solid.

Until the next day, when nature sets the bright January sun shining onto the beach cottage. Onto the roof, in particular. And that frozen snow-pack melts a

99

little beneath those rays—except the clogged gutters block the melted snow from dripping away.

And so it drips instead through the roof, and ceiling, down into that silver pot set beneath it.

Until Mack finally picks up a roof rake—though it is hard to come by—and he gets that whole roof cleared off. And no more melting snow leaks through the living room ceiling of the beach cottage.

～

For a while, until that ceiling stain dries out, Mack and Avery still do look up at it—night after night. They look at that stain as logs burn in the fireplace, and as the wind whistles outside, and as snow flurries tap-tap at the windowpanes, and as Avery scuffs around in her robe and fluffy slippers. Even later each evening, as Avery turns on the living room lamp, and as Mack reads her a chapter from the novel she'd brought along, their glances occasionally venture to that ceiling stain.

Hours pass *without* a ceiling glance, though. Hours when Mack leaves for Martinelli Upholstering's warehouse, where he measures chairs and cushions and pillows, and cuts fabrics, and tufts a seatback, and handles virtual customer consultations. And hours when Avery works in the cottage sewing room. With the sewing machine moved aside, her window-display mocks are strewn across the long table. Her laptop is open as she video-chats with coworkers.

But still, when Avery and Mack come in from winter walks in this two-hundred-acre nature preserve hidden by forest and edged by sea and accessible by one winding dirt road, and as they stamp off their boots and hang their coats and scarves on hooks, their eyes do wander up to that stain on the living room ceiling.

Something else is happening, too, at the same time.

Avery Martinelli breathes easier. They always leave a cottage window open a crack, and during those January days, salt air comes in; haunting cries of winter birds do, too. Foghorns and bell buoys join the sounds. And friendly neighbor hellos come in, as do random snowflakes blowing in with the breeze off the sea.

But most of all, it seems, love comes in.

Maybe that ceiling stain that started from the neglected, clogged gutters grows a little bigger those early days, but comfort grows, too, as families in surrounding cottages are cozy in *their* homes—all of which have lights on those January evenings.

And Mack? Well. He finally places an order for a can of ceiling paint. Afterward, he digs around in his down-vest pocket and finds his father's crumpled task list. Bending over the kitchen counter, he smoothes the piece of paper and adds *Paint Ceiling* at the bottom— underlining the words twice. Tells Avery, too, that when the paint is delivered? He'll take a day off work and get the ceiling all fixed up.

〜

101

A few days later, the cottage living room is a mess. Furniture is moved aside. Drop cloths are set out on the wood floor. A stepladder is opened beneath the ceiling stain, and a tray of white paint is set on the ladder's swing-out shelf. A work light is plugged in over in the corner, near the white sofa. The light shines a bright beam on the ceiling. A painting extension pole, with a roller attached to the end, leans against a nearby wall.

Wearing a sweatshirt over fleece joggers, *and* holding a paintbrush, Mack climbs the ladder. There, he meticulously does a little touch-up painting on the discolored ceiling—cutting in around the edges of the stain, blending the new paint with the existing ceiling paint. Tipping up the brim of his white painter's cap, he leans back and eyes the stain, right as Avery's voice calls out—loud and clear—from the kitchen.

"Mack Martinelli! Don't tell me you used the very last paper towel!" Without much of a pause, she goes on. "Whoever uses the last paper towel is supposed to replace it with a new roll. From the pantry! No one can dry their hands or wash a dish or wipe a counter—with *this*!"

As she says it, Avery stomps through the cottage while clutching a cardboard paper towel tube. And giving it a good shake. She's wearing a long, gray duster sweater over black skinny jeans frayed at the hem; studded suede booties are on her feet; her hair is twisted into the piecey side braid she's been favoring.

And she's making a beeline straight for Mack.

Hurrying through the dining room; passing the half-finished jigsaw puzzle on the table there; sidestepping the living room coffee table, where a board game is set up; glancing at the logs stacked near the fireplace—beside which last night's wineglasses still sit—Avery approaches Mack just as he looks down at her from the stepladder.

Which seems the perfect time for her to give his leg a good swatting with that empty paper towel tube. Oh, but if you look closely enough, there's no missing the twinkle in her eye and smile on her lips, too.

No, there's no missing how she'll use any reason to be near Mack, to talk to him, to watch him. Because watch him she does—as he sets his paintbrush on the paint tray and descends that stepladder, one rung at a time, before turning to her.

"*Mack*," she whispers while stepping closer, still holding that ragged cardboard tube. She also nudges up his painter's cap and draws her fingers along his whiskered jaw.

Mack takes that tube from her, wraps his arm around her shoulder, pulls her even closer and gives his—somewhat—indignant wife a long kiss. His arm holds her tight as she deepens that kiss. Deepens it enough for Mack to drop that paper towel tube, then cradle her neck with that now-empty hand. It's obvious he doesn't want to let go of her as much as she doesn't want him to.

He does, though. It happens when Avery whispers into that kiss, *"Don't you know you're supposed to replace the paper towels?"*

Slowly, Mack pulls back, strokes her messy side braid, kisses her once more and says, "Okay, Mrs. Martinelli. I'll learn."

Next—journey into

THE
SEASIDE SAGA

A book series following a group of
beach friends on the Connecticut shore.

FROM NEW YORK TIMES BESTSELLING AUTHOR

JOANNE DEMAIO

The Seaside Saga

Reading Order

For a complete list of books by *New York Times* bestselling author Joanne DeMaio, visit:

Joannedemaio.com

About the Author

JOANNE DEMAIO is a *New York Times* and *USA Today* bestselling author of contemporary fiction. The novels of her ongoing and groundbreaking Seaside Saga journey with a group of beach friends, much the way a TV series does, continuing with the same cast of characters from book-to-book. In addition, she writes winter novels set in a quaint New England town. Joanne lives with her family in Connecticut.

For a complete list of books and for news on upcoming releases, visit Joanne's website. She also enjoys hearing from readers on Facebook.

Author Website:
Joannedemaio.com

Facebook:
Facebook.com/JoanneDeMaioAuthor

Made in the USA
Monee, IL
12 September 2021